The Haunting of Lost Souls House

CAT KNIGHT

©Copyright 2020 Cat Knight

All Rights Reserved

Disclaimer

This story is a work of fiction, any resemblance to people is purely coincidence. All places, names, events, businesses, etc. are used in a fictional manner. All characters are from the imagination of the author.

Table of Contents

Disclaimer..*iv*

Prologue *1*

Chapter One...*11*

Chapter Two *21*

Chapter Three *29*

Chapter Four *39*

Chapter Five..*49*

Chapter Six *57*

Chapter Seven...*67*

Chapter Eight *77*

Chapter Nine...*87*

Epilogue..*103*

PREVIEW...*111*

   THE HAUNTING OF COVEN CASTLE *111*

Prologue *113*

About the Author *121*

RECEIVE THE HAUNTING OF LILAC HOUSE FREE!
....*122*

Prologue

"It's your turn."

Jeremy looked at his older sister and put his hands behind his back. "I don't want to."

"Don't be silly," Lisbeth said. "You know you want to."

She held out the magnifying glass, as if it were some sort of Sherlock Holmes prop.

Jeremy shook his head. "I don't want to. You do it."

"I did it already."

Jeremy looked around the attic, as if trying to find a way out. It was a small attic over a small house. The usual flotsam and jetsam of daily life was all about. Boxes were stacked to one side, where the steep roof kept everyone at bay. In another corner stood the excess lamps and luggage. Next to that little pile were the old tennis racquets and golf clubs no one could bring themselves to throw away. Dusty, quiet, it was the perfect playroom for Jeremy and his sister.

Their mother often sent them to the attic to play, while she "entertained" in the parlour. They didn't understand the full meaning of "entertain", but they were only nine and eight.

And they didn't mind being in the attic. No one bothered them there. The window provided enough light for games and reading, and when the sun shined, the room filled with light—like this day.

"Go on," Lisbeth said. "It's educational."

Jeremy frowned.

"We're learning about paper and fire, and that's educational."

"Jeremy looked at the jar filled with slips of paper. "I don't see why we have to do it more than once."

"Because it's not science if you do but once," Lisbeth said. "If the experiment cannot be repeated, then it's just luck or something. You'll learn about that next year."

"But we already know."

"We think we know. Besides, it's wickedly fascinating, isn't it?"

Jeremy looked from the jar of paper to the magnifying glass. "It is fascinating." He held out his hand, and Lisbeth handed over the magnifying glass.

"You have to get it focused just right," she said.

"I saw you do it. I know how."

Jeremy moved around so the sunlight was over his right shoulder. Then, he held the magnifying glass in the beam of sunshine, focusing it into a tiny point that he aimed through the glass, directly at a slip of white paper.

The paper did nothing.

Lisbeth giggled. "It takes a bit of time."

Jeremy carefully held still the focused beam, and even as he did, the paper began to brown.

They both laughed as the paper suddenly burst into flames.

"One more," Lisbeth said. "See if you can light another."

Jeremy frowned as he sought to keep the hot point on a slip of paper. With smoke accumulating inside the jar, it wasn't easy.

"Here, let me," Lisbeth said and snatched the magnifying glass. "Like this."

Her face grew stern as she put the beam on the paper. The beam was steady, and in a few seconds, the paper began to brown. A few more seconds, and flames appeared.

Jeremy clapped.

"That's how you do it," Lisbeth said.

"Let me try, let me try," Jeremy begged.

"Hold out your hand," Lisbeth said.

"Why?"

"Just do it, silly."

He held out his hand, and she grabbed his wrist. "Hold still."

With a smile, Lisbeth pulled his hand into the light beam, and it took but seconds to use the glass to focus the beam on Jeremy's hand.

"How does that feel?" she asked.

"Hot," he replied. "Ouch," he jerked away his hand.

She laughed.

"Now, you know how the paper feels."

Jeremy rubbed the back of his hand, even as a tear came to his eye.

"Baby," Lisbeth said. "Can't take a spot of pain?"

"You try it," he said. "Let's see how you make out."

Lisbeth put her hand into the beam and used the glass to turn the beam into a ray. Jeremy watched as she held her hand there for some seconds, far longer than he had. When she finally jerked away her hand, there was a deep red spot where the ray had burned her.

"See," she panted. "That's how you do it."

"I want to do another," Jeremy said.

She handed over the glass and licked her hand.

"We're going to start them all on fire, aren't we?"

"All of them," she said. "All of them."

The attic provided days and nights of fun for Jeremy and Lisbeth.

They didn't need the sun for some of their "experiments". There was the rabbit experiment that required more than a bit of daring, as they had to pinch the small rabbit from the hutch three houses away. That was a daring, nighttime hike, while their mother was "entertaining" in her bedroom. There was so much commotion coming from the bedroom, that Jeremy and Lisbeth didn't have to be particularly stealthy, not until they left the house.

Moving about in the dark was not anything new either. They sometimes liked to roam about. Together, they had little fear of the dark, even without a torch. When they went out to pinch something, they never used a torch.

The doll came from the house three lots away. It belonged to a little girl named Lottie, and it was nice doll. Jeremy and Lisbeth hadn't gone to Lottie's house to steal the doll. It just happened to be left out in the open. And well, they didn't like Lottie, not at all. Lisbeth was the one who actually sneaked up to the patio and the table. She was the one that grabbed the blonde-haired doll and skipped back to Jeremy.

"Let me hold it," Jeremy said.

"In a bit," she answered. "When we get back."

"I won't drop it. I'll be careful."

"When we get back," she repeated.

"We're going to have fun with it, aren't we?" Jeremy asked.

"Of course, we are," she said.

The children did have to be a bit more quiet when they returned, as the antics in the bedroom had toned down. Still, they no problem stealing into the attic. That was when Lisbeth handed the doll to Jeremy, while she prepared the experiment.

Looping the cord over the rafter was far from easy, but after a few tries, she managed. Jeremy held up the doll, and she looped the cord around the doll's neck. She made it tight, like a leash. Jeremy let go, and the doll swung in the scant light.

"Are you ready?" Lisbeth asked.

Jeremy picked up a cricket bat. "Ready," he announced.

"Wait," Lisbeth said. "What is the doll's name?"

"Lottie," Jeremy answered.

"That's too easy," Lisbeth said. "How about Florence?"

Jeremy giggled. "Florence is mum's name."

She grabbed a tennis racquet. "I think it is appropriate."

Lisbeth stepped up and smiled at the doll. "Florence, you have been very bad."

She smacked the doll, and it swung back and forth. Jeremy laughed.

"My turn," he said. He stepped up and hit the doll with the cricket bat.

"Smashing," Lisbeth said. "Florence has been very, very bad."

They took turns hitting the doll, sending it swinging in all directions. They called the doll "bad" and "mean" and "cruel", as they smashed it. It was great fun, and they laughed.

Lisbeth took a particularly vicious swing, and the doll came apart, its body flying across the room, which delighted Jeremy.

"She's lost her head," he said. "She's lost her head."

Lisbeth laughed too. "I suppose that's what she deserved."

"What's going on up there?" their mum called up the stairs.

Lisbeth held her finger to her lips, and Jeremy covered his mouth with his hand.

"Jeremy was trying to do a handstand and fell over," she called down.

"Is he hurt?"

"No," Lisbeth said. "It was just funny."

"You two need to come down. It's time for bed."

"Yes, mum, we'll be right down."

Jeremy ran over and grabbed the doll's body, which he laid on their small table.

"We need another doll," he said.

A month later, there were five bodyless dolls hanging from the rafters, five bodies on the table. The dolls were of different vintage, size, and age. Not that it mattered to Lisbeth and Jeremy. Pinching the dolls and smacking them was great fun— at least for Jeremy. Lisbeth had grown tired of the game. Dolls were just...dolls.

So, with the darkness seeping in through the window, and Jeremy laughing, and their mum almost shouting, Lisbeth wondered what would happen if she smacked her brother in the head. Since she had the cricket bat, it was easy. She simply wound up and swung...hard.

The THUNK of the bat on Jeremy's head was far different than the bap of the bat on the dolls. And his head didn't fly off, like the dolls. He just dropped to the floor.

"Now, look what you've done," Lisbeth said as she watched the blood leak from Jeremy's head. "You've gone and made a mess. You're being very naughty."

She hit Jeremy again, but not as hard. The THUNK was somehow satisfying, as if playing a drum of some kind.

"Do get up," Lisbeth said. "Stop pretending you're hurt."

Jeremy didn't move.

So, she THUNKED him again.

Lisbeth was losing patience. "Get up, Jeremy," she said and THUNKED him yet one more time.

But Jeremy didn't move, and the nosebleed Lisbeth thought he had didn't stop. She frowned and sat at the table. That was when she thought, perhaps, that she had struck Jeremy too hard.

"He's gone to sleep for a bit," she said out loud. "He'll wake up soon."

She watched, thinking perhaps she should do something about the blood.

Mum would be quite put out about the blood. She needed a towel, and there were no towels in the attic.

"I wish you could be a bit more thoughtful," she said as she stood. "Now, I have to clean up your mess."

She threatened to THUNK him one more time, but she didn't. Instead, she laid down the cricket bat and started for the steep stairs that led down from the attic. As she reached them, she heard, or thought she heard, his voice. She spun quickly, too quickly. She lost her balance and fell backward. Being so close to the stairs, she tumbled down them, and her head SMACKED a riser very hard. That was the last thing she sort of remembered. After that everything went black.

Just as it had for Jeremy.

Chapter One

Ava pulled up the rental listings and reached for her pint. The tablet computer was bigger than her phone screen, but it was still a bit too small to give her a good idea of the property. It was not too small to show her the monthly charge. That was the bugaboo for Ava. She didn't have much money for rent. In fact, she had bloody little. She faced the age-old conundrum of people chasing housing. What she could afford, she couldn't see herself living in. What she could live in, she couldn't afford. She sipped her ale. In the middle of the afternoon, the pub was mostly empty.

That was fine with Ava. At night, the blokes from the bar would be bringing her pints and asking for her mobile number, or offering theirs. The search would be longer and less satisfying. Pints had a way of transforming real work into something better left to tomorrow. She arranged the listings from least expensive to most. She stared at the photos and shook her head. The photos almost made the places look passable—almost. And Ava had to remember that those places would never look better than those pics. After five pages of rejects, she was about to pull out her blonde hair.

Then, she found it.

She found the house, because it was a house.

It was an older house, and it certainly wasn't large, but it was a...house. Bedrooms, kitchen, dining room, family room. And the rent was incredibly affordable. Far cheaper than she thought it should be.

That scared her.

Something was obviously wrong with the house. If there was nothing wrong, then it would rent for much more. She tried to think of all the things that might be wrong with the place. No doubt, it was next to an airport, or train track, or highway. The plumbing probably didn't work. The heater couldn't maintain a constant temperature, and on rainy days, the electricity shorted out. Ava was savvy enough to know that houses didn't rent for what was advertised. Yet, Ava was intrigued. She knew, just knew she had to check out the house, and the sooner the better. If the advert was legitimate, there would be many inquiries. Ava grabbed her phone. Waiting would consign her to one of the small apartments she would share with...bugs.

The house was indeed better than anything Ava could imagine. The house stood by itself, two lots away from the nearest one-story that looked forlorn compared to the two-story Ava wanted to rent.

"It comes fully furnished," the owner said. She was an older woman, whose smile was sweet. Ava had the notion that the owner would find it impossible to lie. Ava knew that was impossible. Everyone told lies.

But some people didn't look as if they could tell lies. She supposed the owner practiced that kind of look. It would be much easier to rent a defective house if one looked like an angel.

Ava liked to remind herself that angels and demons didn't exist. Some people believed in angels and demons and ghosts and all manner of magical beings. Ava thought those people were crazy or stupid or both.

"What's wrong with the house?" Ava asked.

"What?" the owner asked?

"I've been through the listings before, and a place this cheap always comes with issues. What are they here?"

"I assure you there are no defects. Everything works, just like it should. Go ahead and test any of the appliances, the plumbing, whatever. And should you find something that is broken, let me know. I will have a repairman here the next day."

Ava was not so certain that she liked the idea of her landlady keeping a list of handymen on her speed dial. What did that say about the house?

"I will take you at your word," Ava said. "But there must be a reason your rent is less than one might expect."

"To tell the truth, this place is a bit far from everything. I mean, the station is a bit of a walk, as is the pub. I'm sure mobile coverage has improved over the years, but it might still be iffy. So, I have to charge less in order to find renters."

Ava understood what the woman was saying, and it made some sense. But Ava knew more than a few people who would jump at the rent the woman was charging.

"I'll take it," Ava said. "And if there are problems, I'll expect you to fix them right away."

"That I'll do."

With that Ava returned to her flat and prepared to move, never an easy thing. She packed what she had and, while happy, felt a bit of trepidation. She had the idea that the owner was holding back something, some information that would come in handy to know. Knowledge was a precious thing. What had former tenants known? Ava wondered if she could somehow talk to a former renter. She supposed that would be possible, if she put in enough effort. Yet, she didn't really want to look a gift horse in the mouth. If she found a deal-breaker, she would have lost out on the best accommodations she had found in two years of hunting.

"You're actually moving out there?" Celise asked.

Ava looked at her friend and nodded. "It's too good a deal to pass up."

Celise was a woman who never worried about anything. It wasn't that Celise possessed a great deal. Her flat was ordinary. Her job was ordinary. Her clothes were ordinary. Her boyfriend was ordinary. Celise led an ordinary life and never worried about a single aspect of her existence. She claimed she lived one ordinary day at a time, rising at the same time and going to bed at the same time.

Tomorrow was the day that never arrived, and yesterday was the day that couldn't be retrieved. So, she fretted about nothing. Ava thought Celise was the most stable person in London.

"Sometimes, deals too good to be true are too good to be true," Celise said.

Ava sipped her ale. At the bar, the blokes were laughing and talking, loud and hoping to be noticed.

In another half hour, they would start to roam the pub with a pint in hand, looking for a woman who looked thirsty. It was an ordinary evening activity. Not all the blokes would become ambassadors of beer, but some would. Ava would have to smile and turn them away. There were still some details to attend to concerning her new home.

"Well, I want you to come visit," Ava said. "We'll discover the dark underside of this new silver cloud together."

"I will be only too happy to experience this abode of milk and honey," Celise said. "And I'll bring a house-warming gift."

"Nonsense. The house is fully furnished. But if you insist, bring a bottle of wine. After all, I'm renting, not owning."

"You know," Celise said. "There might be other reasons why the rent is so cheap."

"Like what?"

"Well, I'm not one for the paranormal, but perhaps, the house is haunted."

"It is not a castle or keep, Celise," Ava said. "I have it on good authority that ghosts haunt only places that feature a dank, dark dungeon."

"You scoff," Celise said. "But my Bill has a penchant for the supernatural, and he's been all over the country, visiting haunted places. While most of those spots nurture their histories like orchids, putting out a fancy display that has no depth, other locations greet you with cold hatred. He went to a castle in Scotland that he will never visit again."

"Was that the witch castle? The one filled with the tainted souls of a thousand witches?"

"Just one witch, and that witch led Bill down a stone staircase to a room what reeked with evil intent. He didn't stay in the room but ran back up the stairs. And the really strange thing was he could never find those stairs a second time."

"It was a castle. I told you. Castles, manor houses, any place old always has a patron ghost, something frightfully evil and wicked. My house is not so old and doesn't come with a dungeon. So, my ghost will be sweet and benign. I'm certain it will bring me flowers and make me tea in the morning."

They laughed together. Ava held up her glass. "To my new digs and the nicest ghost you'll ever know."

The clicked glasses and sipped.

***

The last night in her flat, Ava experienced separation anxiety. No, that wasn't quite it. She wasn't worried about leaving the flat. She was worried about moving into the house. Something about the house didn't feel right.

She told herself she should have asked more about the history of the house. Had anything bad happened there? She supposed bad things happened in almost all houses, but this one gave off a bad feeling. She didn't know what or who or whichever, but it was like touring the Tower of London and discovering just how many people were beheaded there. Bad things left behind some kind of marker, didn't they? People were more than logic. They felt things. Intuition was real. Mothers knew when their children were hurt. Twins felt each other's pain. She had the gut feeling something about the house was wrong. Yet, logic and greed told her that she was being silly. It was a house. Nothing more. Nothing less.

She was moving, and she would be perfectly safe and perfectly happy in her new abode. To think anything less was being a ninny. When morning came, she would check her flat for anything she might have overlooked, lock the door, turn over the keys to the manager, and drive off to the land of space and silence. She promised herself that she would start that wonderful novel that had wandered about inside her head since she was a teenager. It would be a very good novel, dark and mysterious and filled with teenage angst.

Truth be told, Ava had started the writing half a dozen times and never exceeded a single chapter always blaming her lack of outlining for the paucity of output.

One day she would thoroughly outline the story before she set fingers to keyboard. How could she expect to turn out page after page if she had no idea what happened next? Writers worked from outlines, didn't they? She would create the blueprint for a novel and would finish it before the urge to write killed the outline in its infancy.

She promised herself.

Ava found nothing she needed to take the next morning. She locked the door, turned over the keys, and had the manager wish her good luck. Ava didn't believe she would need luck. She had fashioned a fantastic bargain, and that was enough to keep her happy, despite the rain.

Rain.

To Ava, it seemed that every time she made a major change in her life, it rained. When she moved out of her parents' house, it rained. When she moved to her second flat, it rained. When she reported for her second job, the rain fell through fog.

Today, as she drove away from London, it poured. Dark, dreary, cold, it was exactly the kind of day most people avoided. Yet, there was a phrase for what she had to do. Time and tide waited for no one. She wasn't sailing, but she was going some place. Time and tide wouldn't wait for her.

As she pulled up in front of the house, she glanced out through the rain-spattered glass. At the top of the house was a window. Ava supposed it illuminated the attic, an attic she had not toured.

Why was that?

The owner had not offered a tour, and well, Ava hadn't noticed a stairway leading to the attic. She knew there had to be some kind of access. She told herself she would find the access and survey the attic. It might provide extra space for storage, although she didn't see where she would need the space. But wasn't Celise always complaining about her lack of space? Might Ava rent out some of her space?

That wouldn't bring in much, but every pound counted. She supposed storage for hire was out of the question.

The wipers swept away the water, giving Ava a clear view of the attic window, a clear view of a...

Face.

Chapter Two

The rain blurred the face, causing Ava to rub her hand over the inside of the windshield, which did exactly nothing. She had to wait for the wipers to slide across before she could again see the window clearly.

No face.

For a moment, Ava simply stared, as the rain once again blurred away everything. A second later, the wiper cleared the glass.

No face.

She shook her head. "Silly Ava," she said out loud, repeating the name her mum used before she passed away. "Silly Ava." Her mum said it almost every night, when Ava would ask that the light in her bedroom be left on.

Ava had never liked the dark, and she was apt to transform any sound into some kind of intruder or monster, waiting for darkness before attacking. If one could believe all the movies and books, really creepy things lived in the dark, the deep blackness of night.

She believed that humans, by their nature hated the dark—probably why they slept through it. She hated it. She hated it more than she could admit.

"Silly Ava."

Her mum said that right before she turned off the lights, plunging Ava into the quasi-dark. Because there was always some light shining into her bedroom. It might be the moon or the distant streetlight or the light from the hallway. It wasn't much, not nearly enough, but it was something. Ava had no idea how awful complete darkness would be. She imagined it would be the worst thing in the world. She imagined it would be an invitation for some creature to take her very soul. In her flat, she used a night light, like a child, in her bedroom. She told herself it was because she sometimes had to rise in the middle of the night to use the loo. But that was a lie. She wanted the night light because it was...light. It was the slayer of the dark. And that was enough.

Ava waited for the rain to subside a bit. Since there was no garage, she didn't fancy running through the rain to the front door. With her luck, her key wouldn't work, and she would get soaked as she tried to unlock the bloody thing. No, she would wait a moment. After all, she was in no hurry. She had the whole weekend to unpack the boxes that would arrive the next day and the whole weekend before she had to go back to work.

The drive to the train station wouldn't take long, and the ride into London was easy. Ava almost relished the train ride, as it would provide time for her to do the things she wanted to do, not the things she had to do. There wouldn't be the chance to sleep quite so much, but sleep was over-rated and Ava was not so young anymore. She needed to produce some work.

The rain pelted her car and glass, and she turned off the engine. No need to waste gas. Through the rain, the house looked wavy and distorted, as if in a dream. In a way, she was living a dream. She had never expected any place half so nice. She could wait to get inside and start her first fire in the fireplace. That would take the chill off a rainy day. That would make the sacrifice worthwhile. A glass of wine and a fire. She sounded like one of those advertisements she saw on the telly, one that made a small house in some quaint town sound like heaven on earth. It would be nice, the fire and all.

The rain eased, and it was time to make a run for the front door. Looking out at the drizzling rain Ava wished she had had the forethought to add an umbrella to her car. Wishes, however, wouldn't do. Grabbing her purse, Ava opened the car door, slid out, and ran for the front door. The rain was enough to bother her, but it wasn't a downpour. She reached the door, and to her delight, the key worked perfectly. Inside thirty seconds, she was safe inside and made a mental note to make sure that she kept an umbrella in the car. Shaking out her coat, she immediately switched on the entry light. Ava was no lover of shadow, let alone darkness.

For the next fifteen minutes, Ava went through the house, turning on lights mostly.

The kitchen, her bedroom, the living room, her office, making certain everything worked. Ava had a habit of extravagance with using lights and while she didn't expect a large bill, she was never exactly frugal. Better to have peace of mind with a well lit house. If it cost her too much, she would adjust her usage until she was used to the house although she doubted she would ever rid herself of the night light. That was one of those "must have" items.

Ava was about to change into her jammies, when she realized that she didn't have any food in the house and that meant she needed to find a pub, as she liked pub food much more than preparing her own. A Glance out the window, confirmed the rain had all but stopped, being reduced to a mist, - to be followed by a fog, if she knew her England. Leaving the lights on, she grabbed her purse and coat and headed out. The nearest village had to have a pub. It was a law, wasn't it? Well, she was pretty sure, it wasn't a real law, just an unwritten one.

Probably devised by wives.

That struck her as funny. Every city, town, and village had to have a pub, a place where women could send their men. Without the pub, the men would stay home, and that was the worst of all worlds for the women. Men needed to be away at times, for some time. Women knew that intrinsically. So, Ava knew she would find a pub, and one pub was much like another. STAFFORD ARMS was such a pub, with a table at the back, where she could eat in peace—for a while.

"Hallo, you're new here."

Ava looked up, and the bloke grinned, a pint in each hand.

"Would you like a pint?" he asked.

"Yes," she said. "Please sit."

He shook his head and set down the pints. "I wasn't expecting you to just say yes." He sat. "I'm Archie."

"Well, Archie, thank you for the pint. But I've found that if I accept the first pint, the other blokes stay away."

He laughed. "That is a good strategy, ain't it? Well, that sits just jack with me. I get to enjoy your company, while the others gape with envy."

"If you give away my secret, you will never sit with me again."

"That means I'll get to sit with you again?"

"If you're first."

"Well, now, that's great. So, you're new. I know, because I'm here probably more often than I should be. Are you living around here, or are you just passing through?"

"I rented a house just outside the town. So, I suppose I'll be coming in often enough."

"I will be on the lookout. By the way, I install Internet and wi-fi equipment in the area, so if you need something, give me a call." He took out a card and passed it over.

"Thanks," she said. "I might need your help. By the way, if I needed wi-fi where I would put the router?"

"Depends. Two story house?"

"Yes, and since I use my laptop all around the house, I need the widest coverage."

"If it was me, I'd put it in the attic. That way it feeds the entire house."

"What if I don't have any power up there?"

"You need to check it out. If you have a light, then you have power. And a router doesn't require much juice."

"Interesting. And the equipment will be all right up there?"

"It's not open to the elements, is it?"

She shrugged. "I haven't been up there."

"Well, you need to take a look. If it's closed to the outside, it's no problem at all. In fact, the equipment will need nothing at all. Once installed, you can forget it."

"That's great. So, I need to do some exploring."

"Apparently. Need help?" He grinned, and Ava did notice that he was a rather handsome bloke.

"Not at the moment," she said. "But I'll keep you in mind."

"I'll give you some advice. Don't hire the cable company to do the work. It's not that they won't do a good job. They will, but they'll charge double what I will. You want to save a few quid, you call me."

"That's good to know. So, you say you're a regular here, who are the blokes to avoid?"

He leaned back. "You're askin' me to put the finger on some of the others?"

"You want to sit in that seat again, don't you?"

"That I do. All right, I'll give you the names of those I wouldn't let my enemy's sister have a go with."

"That's a good beginning."

"Aye, the best. Well, steer clear of Rodney. He's a smooth talker but likes to use a woman's credit cards, if you know what I mean."

"Indeed, I do," Ava said. She leaned back and listened. She was certain that Archie would give her more information than she could remember, but that was fine. She next bloke might be the one that said she had to avoid...Archie.

On the ride back to the house, Ava reviewed the advice she had received from Archie. It was more than a bit obvious that she needed to find access to the attic and take an inventory. She supposed she could call her landlady and ask, but the hour was late. Certainly, the attic access couldn't be that hard to find. She was surprised she hadn't found it already. If she couldn't find it, she would contact the landlady. Enough said.

The lights in the house made her smile. She parked her car and stopped to look. Not every room was lit, but the ones that were lit cheered her. Locking the front door behind her, Ava closed her eyes and took a deep breath. This was exactly what she needed. Quiet, close, warm, the best abode she had ever known—outside where she grew up.

Giggle.

Her eyes popped open, and Ava looked all about.

Giggle?!

She stared. She knew she had heard a "giggle", a child's giggle. But she couldn't have. There were no children in the house. As far as she knew, there had never been any children in the house. She shook her head. She couldn't have heard what she thought she heard. That was impossible, so her ears needed cleaning or something. No, no, that wasn't it. The noise in the pub had affected her ears. Of course, her ears would return to normal by morning.

It was like going to a concert, where the band used fifteen-foot amps that made everyone's ears ring. Pubs could be like that also. So, her ears had been affected and nothing else. There was no giggle, not child. There was only a misbehaving ear.

Had she picked up some sort of germ?

Was she coming down with a cold?

She didn't feel feverish, but then, she had had two pints. So, she wasn't feeling any discomfort anywhere. She chuckled and pushed herself for the stairs. As she went, she turned off the lights she had turned on previously. In the kitchen, she made sure the back door was locked. She thought she had heard a child's giggle, but it could have been anyone's giggle. So, making sure the house was secure was important. Satisfied she proceeded to her bedroom. She stopped in the middle of the room and listened.

Nothing.

Blissful nothing.

Ava smiled. She had the feeling that despite the ale-generated giggle, she was going to be just fine. The house would more than do, it would be a refuge. As she slipped under the covers, she reminded herself that she had one important task for the next day, shad to find the attic access, and she had to examine the attic. Then, she could call Archie and hire him to set up her wi-fi. She smiled as she fell asleep.

Giggle.

Chapter Three

Ava's eyes popped open, and she sat up in bed. The night light provided enough illumination to look about the room. She saw no one, certainly not a child, for she was certain it was a child's giggle. She shivered and waited, her heart suddenly racing in her chest.

A child's giggle.

She had heard it. The child had to be in the room.

But where?

She looked about and wondered if she had actually heard the giggle. Might it have been some bit of a dream, some imagined sound? That made sense. It was nothing more than her imagination.

She concentrated. She had been asleep, well, not fully asleep. She was in that nether world between sleep and wakefulness. In that boundary area, she couldn't be certain about anything. And since she had been thinking about the giggle before she tried to sleep, didn't it make sense that her mind had conjured up another giggle?

Wasn't it true that peopled dreamed about the last thing they considered before sleep overwhelmed their minds?

Of course, she was almost destined to hear a giggle. She could hardly avoid it. A new bedroom, with new sounds, in a new house, she wondered why she hadn't heard full dinner conversations. It probably wasn't even a giggle. It was probably her tummy processing the ale. Her dream-wrapped mind had transformed a rather ordinary stomach gurgle for some sort of childish giggle. That was the real explanation. Her brain had misinterpreted the plain. She chided herself for being so eager to think a child was in the room. She was just being childish, silly.

Giggle.

Ava looked about. One giggle might be a dream. The second meant something else—unless she was willing to accept some sort of hallucination. If there was a child, then it was in the room. She slipped out of bed and knew that the child could be under the bed or in the loo or closet. There was nowhere else to go. To make sure, Ava went to the door and locked it. She flipped on the overhead light and dropped to her knees on the carpet. She looked under the bed.

Empty.

That left the loo or the closet.

She pulled the loo door shut, listening to the creak of old hinges. That pleased her. No one could go in or out without making noise. Then, she reached in and turned on the closet light. She waited in the doorway, as if the child were going to charge past her.

The closet wasn't that big, but a child could hide behind the clothes, back in a corner.

"Come out," Ava said out loud. "I won't hurt you."

She received no reply, which bothered her a bit. Then, she dropped to her knees again to look under the clothes for small feet.

Nothing.

She stood and remembered to look above the clothes, as if the child had climbed onto a shelf.

Nothing.

Frowning, she backed out and turned off the light. The closet door also creaked as she closed it. That was fine. The creak was some sort of early-warning system. No one could go in or out without her knowing.

That left the loo.

She took a deep breath and opened the loo door, hearing the creak. Fine with her. She flipped on the light and entered.

No one.

She stepped to the shower curtain and the moment of truth. It was the last place in the bedroom where the child could hide—the last place. Grabbing the curtain, she pulled it back, like some magician exposing the contents of the torture box.

No one.

Ava stood staring and wondering. She knew she had heard giggles.

But had she?

Probably not. It was probably just some sort of sound from somewhere that made her think of a child's giggle. She would pursue it in the morning.

She turned off the lights as she headed for bed—all but the night light. She needed a bit of backup, something to reassure her. Shaking her head, she closed her eyes and let sleep come. It wasn't long. And there were no more giggles.

Ava luxuriated in the morning light. She smiled and listened and heard nothing but some birdsong outside. That was a welcome change from her flat. Traffic noise had been her morning alarm at the flat. She almost laughed. She knew this house would perfect for her. She put on a robe and practically skipped down to the kitchen for tea, there was no waking up without tea. While she sipped, she checked her mobile for messages and news. What popped up was something about a new virus, a scary thing that had started in China and was spreading everywhere. She wondered if she should run to the town and get a paper. No, she wasn't going to do that. She was pretty sure the cable was working, so she would set up the Beeb and get all the news she could stomach.

Of course, the Beeb came after she found the door to the attic.

Taking her cup with her, Ava started on her hunt, and the logical place for a door to the attic was on the second floor. After looking along the hall and not finding any access, not even in the ceiling, she surmised that logic wasn't all it was cracked up to be.

She went from bedroom to bedroom and looked for a door or ceiling access. She checked the closet and loo ceilings. Pull down steps would work, but she found nothing.

Ava grumbled to herself There had to be access to the attic. Every house would have a way to get up there. Where could it be?

First floor?

Ava wasn't convinced the first floor would provide the access, but she looked anyway. After freshening her cup, she took a tour of the first floor, checking behind every door for stairs that would lead to the attic.

Nothing.

She did find some dust bunnies and a few dead insects, things to be vacuumed up later, but she did not find stairs. That made her frown, fix yet one more cup of tea and walk down into the basement. No sane house builder would start the stairs for the attic from the basement, she didn't think, but builders were known to be eccentric types. So, she looked. She found no steps.

Taking a walk around the house Ava looked for an outside access to the attic. Some houses did have outside stairs, especially if they took in boarders. Ava wasn't interested in boarders, but she felt the need to pursue all avenues of access. The outside proved as empty as the rest of the house. She returned to the kitchen, sat, and thought about the problem. Did she really have no way to reach the attic? Picking up her mobile, she called her landlady.

"I hate to sound like a ninny," Ava said. "But how exactly do I get to the attic?"

"Oh, yes, that," the woman said. "The bedroom farthest away from the staircase. At the very back of the closet, there is a door. It doesn't look like a door because there is a shoe cabinet attached. I suppose the builder thought the door could serve as a wall, since it wouldn't be opened very often. To the side of the cabinet, there is a doorknob and a lock. The steps behind the door lead to the attic. But there's nothing up there. Why do you want to see it?"

"I think I might need to put a router up there to improve my wi-fi. There is electricity to the attic, isn't there?"

"Yes, two bare bulbs and several outlets."

"Perfect, and thank you so much."

"You're more than welcome."

Ava detected a hint of hesitation in the landlady's voice, as if there was something amiss with the attic. Well, that might not be the landlady. That could be Ava remembering the face in the window. Naturally, she would add a bit of mystery to the attic. Who wouldn't?

The door to the attic steps was exactly where the landlady said it was, only the door had two locks, not one. That seemed like overkill to Ava. What could possibly come down the stairs? Perhaps there had been a time when someone stayed up there? Some crazy uncle? Wouldn't that make an excellent tale to share with her friends. Yes, poor, poor Uncle Albert had to be sequestered in the attic, lest he molest the toads in the pond, or something like that.

Ava supposed that in the days before modern group homes, crazy relatives had to be locked away in some fashion. She unlocked the door and swung it open.

Inside the door was a light switch, and true to her nature, she turned on the lights. That was pleasing. She climbed the narrow stairs, wondering how anyone might use the attic for storage. Nothing too big could be handled. She reached the top and looked down the length of the room.

And froze.

The doll head hung in the exact centre of the room. At the end of a short rope, the head stared at Ava, just the head. Ava shivered, wondering what had happened to the body, and who had hung the head. She found she couldn't move. She looked into the blue doll eyes that showed no life whatever, eyes that belied the doll's little smile, small dimples. Blonde hair hung over the doll's ears, and Ava was certain that at one time, the doll would have made some young girl happy. Ava, herself, had owned such a doll, a doll to play house with, a doll to talk to.

But Ava had always kept the doll head attached to the body. And she had never hung her doll as if imitating some unholy gallows.

She wondered who had hung the doll? She didn't believe it could a young girl who owned the doll. Maybe it was a brother... yes, it most likely would have been the slightly off brother of a poor hapless girl who thought hanging the doll's head would scare his sister. Yes, that made sense. The boy would be the menace. He would be the one bored to death by rain or snow or something.

A little terror, he would have torn head from body and hung the head for his sister to see and scream. Boys always did that. If it wasn't a doll, it was a toad down a sister's shirt or a spider in a jar. Boys lived to scare girls. It was one of life's little mysteries.

Shaking her head, Ava walked to the doll and wondered how long it had been hanging there. She supposed she could ring up the landlady and ask how long it had been since there were children in the house, but she didn't see any real need to know. She knew that she could not reach the rafter from which the doll hung. She would need a stool or stepladder for that. So, she merely untied the head, which felt decidedly ghastly. For some reason, she didn't wish to touch it. It felt cold and oily in her hand. Age might have done that. She tossed the head into a corner, and she didn't really know why. She supposed she should take it down and toss it in the rubbish bin. But she didn't want to pick it up.

She took a step for the doll head and stopped. No doubt, she could get Archie to toss out the head. That made sense. No need for her to handle it. In fact, she was certain she could get Archie to take down the rope also. Her problem was solved. All she had to do was call him. The bloke would come running. As she descended the stairs, she congratulated herself on discovering the attic and making sure it was suitable for whatever equipment Archie might install. The attic was warm enough and dry enough and empty enough. She was on a roll.

Now she needed a shower.

She was basking under the hot water when she heard it.

Giggle.

Despite the heat, Ava felt a surge of cold. She stared at the curtain, because the giggle had come from the other side. It was a child's giggle, the same giggle she had heard the night before. She would swear to that.

But there couldn't be a giggle because she was alone in the house with the doors locked. The telly wasn't on, and her laptop was safe in its case. So, she reasoned she was hearing things that couldn't be.

Just on the other side of the curtain.

All she had to do was pull the curtain a wee bit aside and look.

All she had to do was face the child that had...giggled.

Dripping water, she bit her lip and gripped the edge of the curtain. The water ran. Steam rose about her. She took a deep breath and pulled back the curtain...just a little.

Chapter Four

The room was empty. Water from Ava's hair dripped on the floor. She stared, as if staring would somehow make a child appear. She didn't know which was worse, a child? Or no child? She shivered despite the hot water. It was just wrong. She was hearing things, and she didn't know why. It was bonkers. She closed the curtain and closed her eyes. She wanted to stand under the hot water for an hour. She wanted to somehow unhear what she had heard. She wanted to think her brain was not slipping into some kind of diseased state. People who heard things weren't stable. In fact, they were precisely the people who became serial killers and homeless people living in tents and pushing about their worldly goods in a trolley. She couldn't be hearing things.

After the shower, Ava pushed aside the giggle and grabbed her mobile and the card she had received the night before. Archie answered on the second ring and promised to stop by that afternoon. Did she need a router? A booster? A mode? He would bring everything, and before the day was through, she would have telly and wi-fi. That was enough for her.

While she waited, she decided to do some additional cleaning, as she had discovered some things while looking for access to the attic. She grabbed her vacuum and started with the downstairs.

Ava had completed her cleaning by lunch, and since she still did not have any food, she was forced to leave the house. She skipped the pub and went to the grocery, where she bought the staples she needed. If she spent a tad more than she intended, it was all right. She would save by not eating out so often. It was in the store that she overheard some ladies talking about that terrible virus that was ravaging the Italy and moving in on England. Ava shuddered. There was always some sort of epidemic sweeping through Asia, or Africa, or America but this was a bit different. They generally didn't sweep through areas so close to home. But, the tabloids loved a good medical story, and it sounded like it could be a bad flu. Tabloids loved any reason the bash the NHS, as if they needed a reason. Ava made a point of steering clear of medical facilities. That was where people picked up illnesses and died.

Ava ate lunch on the patio. She had to haul a chair from the kitchen, and she made a mental note to call her landlady and inquire about patio furniture. Still, the day was pleasantly warm and sunny, and the view, while spectacular was good enough. She left the chair on the patio, as she thought she might have her afternoon tea there.

While she waited for Archie, she started on the outline for her novel. She had read somewhere that most would-be novelists never knew what to do with a rainy Sunday afternoon. Well, she knew how she would spend her spare hours. She would outline her Gothic romance.

In her estimation, the book might become more horror-thriller than romance, but that was part of the Gothic formula, wasn't it? There had to be a monster hanging around somewhere in the story. Her quest was for a monster that would be scary enough without being triumphant. Readers simply wouldn't abide a monster who couldn't be killed.

Archie arrived at the appointed time, and he was all smiles as he walked into the house.

"I know this place," he said. "But I've never been inside. Show me the attic?"

"This way."

As they walked up to the bedroom and the hidden, closet access, Archie told her about his day, how he managed to get service for a little, old lady who had given up her house in favour of a flat. She didn't understand a single thing he said or did, but as soon as the remote worked, she was happier than a pig in mud. As long as she could watch her game shows and some reality thing about old couples traveling about the world, she would be happy.

"Two locks?" Archie asked when he saw the door.

"I don't know why either," Ava said. "Up you go."

"Coming with?"

"No, I'm working. And mind the doll's head. Just put that in your rubbish bag."

"Doll's head?"

"The renters before me left a doll's head up there, and I didn't have time to grab it up. Oh, there's a rope hanging from a rafter too. If could detach that, great."

"As you wish. I'll be back in a jiffy."

Archie was back in a few minutes. He joined Ava in the kitchen.

"No real problem," he said. "A good place for a booster router. Plenty of power and such. But I couldn't find the doll head. Are you sure about that?"

"I thought I was," she said. "And the rope?"

"That will come down as soon as I get my step stool up there. Now, show me where the tellies are going to be."

Ava showed Archie where she wanted the tellys, and he made a note of what he would need. Then, she returned to the kitchen, wondering about the doll's head. Surely, he hadn't missed it, had he? After all, there was nothing in the attic but the doll's head and rope. So, either he was lying, or he hadn't really looked.

Then, it hit her.

He had found the doll's head, and he had probably reattached it to the rope, with the hope that she would go to the attic and find it. He would, no doubt, hee-haw when she was scared to death. It was exactly the sort of trick she expected from a bloke like Archie. Make the little lady scared. Then, she'll jump into big, strong arms, to be comforted. Like bloody hell. She wasn't going to play that game. If he said the doll's head wasn't there, then it wasn't there. She would be cool about it.

It took two hours for Archie to complete his work, two hours she spent with her Gothic romance. She was happy for the break.

"Did you hear about the virus?" Archie asked as he showed her how the telly worked.

"Yes, it's all over the place isn't it. Isn't it just a new flu?"

"Something a bit different, I think. And it's spreading into London, if you can believe it. They say it's bad."

"Bad-bad, or just bad?"

"Bad-bad, I suppose. The public health people are saying it will spread like fire and perhaps kill off a few."

"If it doesn't, hospital will."

Archie laughed. Then, he showed her how the wi-fi worked, having her take her laptop from kitchen to bedroom to check the reception.

"It should be right as rain," he said. "A strong signal everywhere. Do you need to see what I've done in the attic?"

"No, I don't think so," she said. That he wanted her to see his work meant he wanted her to find the doll's head and be afraid.

"Good enough," he said. "I took down the rope and left it on the floor. Not much, but spare rope, even old, spare rope is good to have around. Comes in handy. By the way, would you like to have dinner later at the pub?"

Ava had been expecting the invitation, and she knew she owed him for the quick and through service.

"Certainly," she said. "I'll meet you there."

"Works for me. We'll share a pint or two."

A bit more chat, and Archie whistled as he left the house. Ava understood. It was part of the cat and mouse game the blokes played. A dinner here, a pint there, and before you knew it, they would be snogging and carrying on. Well, he might think that way, but she was a long way from snogging with Archie, or any other bloke for that matter. She had things she needed to do. The first of which was to take down the stupid doll's head he had left hanging in the attic.

She found the attic door properly locked. She opened the door and felt a rush of cold air. Had Archie left the window open? That wouldn't do, not one bit. She was of a mind to scold him at dinner for such an infraction. She turned on the lights and marched up the steps. As soon as she reached the top, she shook her head.

There exactly where it had been before hung the doll's head, the brown eyes staring at her.

Brown?

Didn't she remember them as blue?

The blonde hair was the same, and the smile was the same, and the dimples were identical. So, she must have misremembered the eyes. Not that it mattered. She looked at the window and found it closed. She walked over to make sure it was locked. As an experiment, she unlocked the window and tried to raise it.

The window wouldn't budge...not for her. Had Archie managed to get it open? Did that explain the coldness?

She shook her head. No matter. The window was stuck or swollen shut or something, and it didn't matter. The doll's eyes didn't matter. She looked over the devices Archie had installed, and the little red lights blinked at her. They were working, and that was all that did matter. She had telly and wi-fi. She was good to go.

She returned to the doll's head and detached it. She would need to come back with a stool to take down the rope, but that was a task for some later date. For now, she was content to take down the doll's head, which again felt incredibly creepy to the touch. She was reminded of the shrunken heads she had seen in the museums, keepsakes brought back from some island where the natives kept such things, shrivelled faces with no eyes. Those things were yucky, and while the doll's head was neither shrunken nor eyeless, it was every bit as yucky. She could barely stand to hold it as she returned to the first floor. In the kitchen, she placed the head in a paper sack and set it on the counter. It would be going with her. She would see Archie's bid and raise it.

Feeling a bit chilled and definitely a bit spooked, she took her tea outdoors. The warm sun welcomed her. She didn't want to sit in the kitchen, where the doll's eyes could see her, well, could see through the sack at her. That thought made her quiver.

In the shower, she waited for the giggle. It never arrived, and she was feeling better as she dressed for the pub. She didn't need to wear anything special. And it was as she was spritzing a bit of perfume that she heard the voice.

" It's your turn."

45

Ava spun and looked. There was a child in the bedroom, as it was a child's voice. There had to be, because the voice was clear as day. She looked about and quickly dropped to her knees to look under the bed.

Nothing.

She rushed to the closet.

Nothing.

Despite the fact she had just come from the shower, she checked the loo.

Nothing.

She returned to the bedroom and bit her lip. She HEARD the voice. She couldn't deny that. But where was the child?

With clenched fists, she left the bedroom and went downstairs for her purse and the sack. She didn't want to look inside the sack to make sure the doll's head was there, but she did. The gruesome little thing made her wince. Why did she hate it so? She hurried to her car, and in no time, she was walking into the pub, purse and sack in hand.

As she supposed, Archie was already in the booth, two pints on the table, and she could see that he had cleaned up for her. Some blokes didn't bother, as if being presentable wasn't important. The smart ones always strived to look their best. Archie even stood as she neared. She could swear he was trying to be a gentleman. He waited till she sat before he took his seat and raised his glass.

"To a nice evening," he said.

She grabbed her glass, and they toasted.

"What's in the sack?" he asked.

"Something I found in the attic. You must have dropped it."

She pushed the sack to him as confusion filled his face.

"I don't remember dropping anything," he said.

"Then, maybe, you simply forgot to pick it up. Go ahead, open it."

He opened the sack, glanced in, and then pulled out the doll's head.

"What the bloody hell is this?"

Chapter Five

"What I asked you to throw away," she said.

"That...that was not in the attic," he said.

"That's where I found it," she said.

"Look, I..." He paused and smiled at her. "I get it. This is your little joke, isn't it? You get to rib me about not doing my job."

Ava shook her head. "I found that hanging from a rafter, at the end of the rope I asked you to take down."

"I did take it down. And the doll's head wasn't there."

They glared at each other, and Ava had the idea that Archie was hanging onto his lie because he couldn't admit his joke had failed. He was the little boy caught in a lie that he couldn't admit to—or the criminal who needed to avoid prison. Some people maintained innocence no matter the evidence.

He put the doll's head in the sack and handed it back. She placed the sack on the floor.

"I swear to you," he said. "There was no doll's head in the attic, and I did remove the rope. If you found the head hanging—"

"I did."

"Then, someone else hung it. Not me. I swear it."

"Swearing won't do."

Ava grabbed the sack and stood. "I think I should leave."

"Because of an old doll's head?'

She stared at him.

"I get it," he said. "I have become unreliable. Is that it?"

"Don't you think that's bad enough?"

"Well, when you think about it, so have you."

Ava knew the conversation wasn't going anywhere, and the evening was over. "Thanks for the drink."

"But you didn't finish it. Stay and finish."

"It's finished."

With that, Ava walked out, taking her sack with her. She thought about leaving it with him, but that would only give him an excuse to come to the house in order to return it. No, she was done with Archie. If she needed more work on her communications, she would find someone else.

At home, she locked the door and immediately poured herself a glass of red wine. She didn't need to ruin her evening just because Archie was a punk. She left the sack on the kitchen counter.

That was something she would get rid of in the morning. She carried the wine up to her bedroom, where she sat in the padded chair and picked up her laptop. Since she had good reception, she might as well catch up on things. As the computer booted, she pulled up her favourite news feed. The headline was rather dire.

GOVERNMENT CONSIDERING LOCKDOWN TO BATTLE VIRUS SPREAD

Ava had never participated in a lockdown of any sort, but she knew just by reading that a lockdown would not only be inconvenient, it would be stifling. She could hardly imagine such a thing.

All because of some new flu?

She shook her head. She could hardly imagine the government being so silly. She could hardly imagine any sort of epidemic so dangerous. She sipped wine and wondered about Archie. No, she wasn't going to give him any thought at all. If he couldn't own up to a simply prank, he wasn't worth a moment's consideration. She had better things to do.

It's your turn.

Ava looked over the laptop. She was certain she was alone, and she didn't want to check under the bed again. So, if she was alone, where did the voice come from? To her way of thinking it came from...her laptop?

She quickly checked the settings to make sure the laptop speakers were turned off. It was just like her to leave them on. Then, when some inane advertisement video popped up, she would hear the voices.

It was something that happened from time to time at work, and the person who forgot to turn off the speakers was always embarrassed. It was like sending an email "reply all" when it was meant to "reply" to a single person. "Reply all" often caused a great deal of trouble.

But her speakers were off.

So, the bleed didn't come from her laptop. It came from...the telly. That made sense. Archie had been tweaking everything. The telly speakers were on, even if the picture wasn't. Or, he had left the system tuned to some radio play. The Beeb played dramas day and night that were filled with telling dialogue. But did she want to leave her cosy bedroom and check the telly? That hardly seemed profitable, given that the dialogue wasn't exactly prolific.

No, it's your turn. I did it last time, remember?

As if on cue, the other voice, the girl's voice filled Ava's ears. Two children from the sound of it, arguing about who's turn it was to scrub the dishes. Ava was well aware of how child disputes played out. It was tit for tat, until some adult came along to settle the dispute. In this case, Ava was the adult who needed to shut down the telly speakers before they drove her crazy. She put down her laptop and left the room in her bare feet. This wasn't a task she enjoyed, but it had to be done.

The bloke doesn't count. He wasn't paying attention.

On the stairs, Ava wanted to tell the children to stop their infernal quarrelling and go to bed. That was what she would have done if the children were real—which they weren't.

Of course, since she didn't have children, she wasn't absolutely sure she would tell them anything. She reached the bottom of the stairs and listened.

Of course, he counts. I did do it.

After he was already gone.

That hardly matters.

Ava had had enough. She stormed into the room and grabbed the remote. In a moment, she had the picture up and the speakers on. She expected some sort of scene with arguing children. Instead, there was a nature show about bats and the spread of this virus. She had no patience for nature shows, especially not nature shows about bats, which she considered the creepiest creatures on God's green earth. They always reminded her of vampires, and she had absolutely fear of them, in fact, maybe she could use a vampire, in her Gothic novel.

Wait.

She stopped and stared at the telly. If there was a nature show playing, with the perfectly modulated voice of a narrator, how did she hear children?

Oh, all right, I'll do it. But I won't like it.

Don't be a baby.

Ava shivered. Where had the voices come from? Was there a second show on the telly? Was that the problem? A cross-bleed of some sort? She was hearing two broadcasts at the same time? Did she know how to check? She was no techie, and she certainly couldn't call Archie.

She was pretty sure he would answer the phone, and he would probably come over, but he wouldn't want to stop at fixing the telly.

No, he would want something more than a pint and a handshake. He was out of the question. How to fix it?

Ava didn't possess a great deal of tech savvy, but she knew enough to pull the plug on her telly. When she did, the nature show disappeared, along with that modulated voice. She stood and listened. If the nature show went away, so should the cross-bleed. After all, the telly speakers were mute. She heard nothing, and she smiled at her ingenuity. The childish prattle had disappeared with the modulated voice.

Do it, already.

Ava froze. The child's voice shouldn't have been heard. But she could hardly unhear it. A tiny fear danced at the base of her brain. Why couldn't she squelch the child's voice? Where was it coming from? How might she get rid of it? She supposed she could cut the power to all the devices, but that would muzzle her communications also. She wouldn't be able to use her laptop or anything—with the exception of her mobile. That risked some rather unfavourable data charges. But she had to get rid of the children, didn't she? And it had to be something coming in over the wires. Nothing else made sense. She stood still, wondering, thinking. She supposed the wine hadn't sharpened her thinking, but there had to be an explanation.

If she could no longer hear the voice, she certain heard the CRASH in the kitchen.

"What the bloody hell," she said as she started for the kitchen. It sounded as if someone had thrown a teapot against the wall.

Ava stepped into the room and immediately saw the problem. Somehow, the teapot had fallen off the counter and shattered when it hit the tile floor. She could see a sea of sharp shards all over the tile. They glittered in the bright light.

"Bloody hell," Ava repeated. The broom and rubbish bin were across the room, which required a bit of fancy stepping. She knew she should fetch shoes for the task, but she could see well enough to avoid everything. Fetching the shoes would only make a simple task something more complicated. Mindful of where she placed her feet, she started through the mine field of shards. She was halfway through when the lights blinked...out.

"What the..." she said and froze. Something more than consternation ran through her. It wasn't enough that the telly was acting up, now, she had a short in the wiring. She wanted to hit something, but she was stuck in the middle of the shard field, waiting for the lights to come on. Because she was pretty sure could neither advance nor retreat without some sort of injury. And the lights had to come back on, didn't they? She looked over her shoulder.

A bit of light shined under the door that led to the dining room. It was something, but it wasn't nearly enough to trust. She tried to remember exactly where she was. Could she reach the cabinets or appliances? No, she was too far away from them.

If she tried to jump, she would probably come up short and make things even worse. But she had to do something. She couldn't wait for morning light. Well, she could, but she didn't want to. She needed to move if those bloody lights weren't going to come back on.

She determined that if she slid her feet slowly, she could manage to push away the shards before they could cut her skin. That made sense, as long as she was patient. So, she carefully pushed one foot forward, feeling the big pieces slide by. Smaller pieces might stay in the seams between the tiles, but she wasn't going to worry about them. She didn't believe they could cause a deep cut. Small slices, she could take care of. She had made a bit of progress and was feeling rather proud of her solution when the CRASH made her jump.

That was a mistake.

She came down on something that sliced into her foot. She felt the quick stab of pain, and she knew what it was.

"BLOODY HELL!" she said.

The lights came back on, and she blinked before she looked at her foot and the growing puddle of blood around it.

Giggle, giggle.

Chapter Six

Ava watched as a rather pretty nurse, wearing rubber gloves and a mask, plucked a shard of teapot from Ava's foot.

"I can close it with sutures, glue, or staples," the nurse said.

"Which is best?" Ava asked.

"If it were me," the nurse said. "I would use sutures. I don't much trust glue in a place that's going to get a lot of pressure."

"Sutures, it is," Ava said.

"Mind telling me how you did this?"

"Well," Ava lied. "I was messing around in the kitchen, in the dark, and I managed to knock the teapot off the counter. Naturally, it shattered, and I was faced with trying to escape without a cut. Obviously, I didn't make it."

"Thought as much," the Nurse said as she swabbed the wound with disinfectant. "You would not believe how many people we see who manage to turn a mishap into some sort of medical issue. Have you had a tetanus booster?"

"I don't recall," Ava said. "Probably. I keep up on that sort of thing."

"Good. But if you find you haven't, let us know. You don't want tetanus."

"My grandfather used to call it Lockjaw. No, I don't want it, sounds dreadful."

"And lethal. You know, you're lucky in a way."

"Lucky to have a cut in my foot?"

"Lucky that we could treat you so quickly. We're expecting an influx of very sick Covid patients. If that happens, we'll all be in gowns and masks, and treating the dying."

"Sounds awful. Is it really that bad?"

"It's happening in up north, in the bigger cities. Just a matter of time before people start dying. Don't go anywhere."

"Where would I go?"

"Who knows? Sometimes, people disappear on us."

"Not me. I need my foot."

The nurse chuckled and left. Ava wondered just how lucky she was. She lived in a house where the wiring needed repair, where voices bled in from the cable connection, and where she still needed to sweep up the shards from a teapot and cup that shouldn't have fallen and shattered. That didn't sound lucky at all. In fact, as she considered it, it sounded outright eerie. Those sorts of things didn't happen in normal houses. A tiny bit of trepidation took hold of her brain. What was wrong with her house?

By the time Ava returned to the house, her foot ached, despite the pain pill the nurse had given her. Only one, since Ava was driving. The numbing shot the nurse had used was wearing off, and despite a plethora of padding and a bandage, Ava found it painful to put any sort of weight on the wound. Yet, she knew she couldn't leave the kitchen a mess. So, as soon as she arrived, she grabbed the broom and swept up the remains of the teapot and cup. She managed but just barely. By the time she finished, her foot throbbed. It was all she could do to pour herself a glass of wine and limp to her bedroom. There, she propped up her foot and took a photo, which she thought would come in handy when she had to call in sick the next day. Although that wouldn't keep her from working. Why else have a laptop?

Giggle.

A chill ran up Ava's spine. She looked about the room. The last thing she was going to do was get up and try to chase down the voice. As long as she didn't face some catastrophe, she would ignore the voices. It was that simple. She would simply put the voices out of her mind. Let them talk all they wanted.

That was good. My turn.

Ava looked about, her eyes darting. She sipped wine, as if the voice meant something more than a show on the Beeb. No, no, no, she told herself. She wasn't going to go down that rabbit hole. In the morning, she would get everything fixed, even if it meant calling Archie. She needn't apologize for the doll's head. She would simply avoid it. He could work without explaining the doll's head.

Doll's head.

Why was that important?

She looked about the room, and her eyes landed on the sack, the sack she had left in the kitchen when she returned from the pub. At least, she was pretty sure she had left it in the kitchen. Now, the sack sat atop her bureau.

Same sack?

It looked the same, the exact same. It was either the same sack or its twin. She knew she should go check, that if she didn't, the sack would nag at her like a sore tooth, or in this case, like her sore foot. But it was a sore foot. She had no ambition to get up and open the sack, because that would make the pain in her foot flare up. The throb had been reduced, thanks to the pain pill, the wine, and the fact that it was propped up at the moment. Why would she increase the pain on purpose? Not for a bloody doll's head. That made no sense at all to her. The doll's head, like the voices, could wait for daylight. Curiosity killed the cat, or so, Ava had always been told.

She pushed the sack out of her mind and returned to the laptop. Sipping wine she looked at the screen.

What should I do?

Get her attention.

Ava frowned. It was almost as if the voices were talking about her.

The lights winked out.

Ava sat in the almost dark. The only light provided by the laptop. She stared, and the small fear inside her head grew.

Surely, that was a coincidence, Ava told herself. Because...because...because it had to be. She sat, her foot propped up, staring out into the mostly dark. Her heart beat faster, as she listened, as she waited. She turned her head slowly from side to side, looking, watching for what might "get her attention". The teapot and cup had been one thing. This was another. The tension ate at her, feeding the anxiety inside. She was one of those movie characters stuck in some impossible place, waiting for the preying monster to arrive. Every second ratcheted up the stress. Every second added to her fear. Her fingers danced about on the keypad, without her even thinking. Her eyes stared. Her ears perked up. What was out there in the dark?

When the doll's head landed in her lap, Ava SCREAMED.

Without thinking, she batted the plastic head away, knocking it as far away as she could. It was as if it was on fire, as if it might send her clothes up in flames. Her heart bounced inside her chest. She fought the urge to jump up and run.

Giggle.

Giggle.

"Who are you?" Ava asked in a quavering voice.

There was no answer. Her good leg bounced nervously. Her fingers mindlessly tapped the keys.

"Who are you?" Ava repeated.

She received no answer. A sudden need to cry bubbled up inside her. No, no, she told herself, she was not going to cry. She was going to think things through.

"Who…" The words died in her throat. Why was she asking the dark who it was? Why would she expect some Beeb show to answer her? That was insane. The show wasn't listening to her. The Beeb didn't know she existed.

"Get…a…grip," she told herself.

She picked up her wine glass and drank the rest. No sipping now, not after the doll's head.

Doll's head.

Ava shook, trembled from head to bandaged foot. The doll's head hadn't come from the telly, not from the Beeb. The voices, yes, the voices might have come from the show, but the doll's head?! No, that shot out of the dark because someone threw it.

She was not alone.

A panic welled up inside Ava. She looked about for some sort of weapon, because she had not doubt that sooner or later, the person in the room would attack. When that happened, she needed a way to defend herself, and bloody screams wouldn't suffice. The only item she had was the wine glass. It wasn't much, but she would bash someone with it, if she had to.

"All right," Ava said. "I know you're there in the dark. So, present yourself. Let's have it."

No one appeared.

"If you don't come out, I swear I'll call the police and have them throw you in jail."

You got her attention.

Now we can have some real fun.

"That does it, you little guttersnipes. The coppers will be here in minutes."

Ava grabbed her phone and dialled the police. Her call was hardly answered in just a few seconds. When it was, she was asked to state her emergency. She told them there were a couple of uninvited bratty kids in her house, causing her all sorts of problems. They were trespassers, and she wanted them removed immediately.

"They're children?" the dispatcher asked.

"Regular imps," Ava answered.

"And you need help in getting them out?"

"I know it sounds ludicrous, but they hide and well, I have a bad foot at the moment."

"Have you been drinking?"

Ava hesitated, but she knew better than to lie. "Yes, a bit of wine, but I assure—"

"I recommend you go to sleep. The little imps will disappear, and you will have the house to yourself. Please, do not call again. Nuisance calls will be prosecuted, especially with the virus upon us."

The connection was severed, leaving Ava flabbergasted.

She had always assumed the police would come, no matter what. Didn't they rescue cats in trees? Didn't they chase away dogs and help little, old ladies across the street? What good were they if they didn't come to chase off two, unruly children? Why was she paying taxes? Anger flashed through her.

"Hear that?" Ava lied to the dark. "The coppers are on their way. So, you two better run away, right now!"

They're not coming.

They never do.

Ava's mouth fell open. She heard no capitulation in the voices, no acknowledgement of their trespass, no wish to run away. What she heard was some sort of calm joy. They were safe, and they knew it. She would receive no help. They were in control, not her. They could do whatever popped into their little heads. That solid confidence scared Ava more than she could admit. She was dealing with a couple of street urchins without a conscience between them.

"When I get up," Ava said. "I'm going to find you. When I do, I'm going to spank you very hard and call your parents. So, if you don't wish to suffer some pain, leave now."

Oh, no, she's going to get up.

Giggle.

The doll's head landed in Ava's lap, and this time, she didn't bat it away. She stared at it, the fear inside mushrooming. What the bloody hell was she fighting? She picked up the doll's head and looked at it. It looked like the one she had taken to the pub, but this one's eyes were...blue.

Wait.

She was certain that the doll's eyes had been brown at the pub.

Hadn't they?

With sudden anger, she threw the doll's head into the dark.

"I've had enough. Turn on the lights."

Turn them on yourself.

Ava set the laptop on the floor, as it provided the only light. She lifted her foot off the stool, and it immediately began to throb. Using her arm, she pushed herself erect. What she needed as a cane, but she didn't have one of those. She waited a moment for her foot to come to some sort of truce with the pain. She grabbed the wine glass and started slowly for the door. She needed to get out of the room. She needed light. She needed to find the little beasts and spank their little arses. Limping, biting her lip against the pain, Ava shuffled along.

The doll's head hit her in the chest, and she jumped.

Then, someone grabbed her ankle, and she fell.

As the hit the floor, she felt the wine glass break.

The broken stem raked along her arm. On the floor, fighting for breath, she felt warm blood on her arm.

Chapter Seven

For some seconds, Ava couldn't move, even though, she knew she had to. She was bleeding, and she needed to fix that. And there was glass on the floor, and she needed to fix that. In the dark, she was not in a position to fix much of anything. She had to get up.

Laugh.

That was fun.

Blood. So nice.

Giggle.

Anger flared, and right behind it was fear, real fear. The urchins were winning. That was obvious, but Ava knew she could win, if she could see them. At the moment, the dark favoured them, but it wouldn't be dark forever. She would find some light, or the sun would rise, and that was when she would make the little monsters pay. She threw the glass stem across the room, where it wouldn't cut her again. Then, she carefully crawled to the door. She pulled herself erect and faced the dark, her laptop still lit by the chair.

"I'll be back," she said. "If you're still here, I'm going to whip you till you won't be able to sit for a week."

Laugh.

Laugh.

Ava opened the door and limped out. The first thing she noticed were the lights, which were on. But she had no faith in the lights. She knew that somehow, the little imps could turn out the lights when it suited them. She needed a torch, and she knew she had one in the kitchen. With the torch, she wouldn't have to rely on the wiring.

She looked at her arm. The cut wasn't bad, but it was still bleeding. It would need binding and some sort of bandage. She wasn't going to bleed to death, and that was a good thing. One hand on the wall, she limped for the stairs, half expecting the lights to go out at any moment. She was happy she wasn't carrying anything that could cut her if she fell. Not that she intended to fall. She reached the stairs and started down, leaning heavily on the railing. Her foot was killing her. Her arm had begun to sting. She felt as if she had done battle with someone. Maybe, she had. Those two children, no, not children, those two bad seeds were in for more than a bit of trouble.

At the bottom of the stairway, she turned for the kitchen. She was glad she had cleaned up the shards of the teapot and cup. As she passed along the hall, she made sure to look into the dark dining room and office. The last thing she wanted was some sort of bushwhacking. She was determined not to be taken unawares again.

What if they weren't imps?

The thought popped into her head, and she frowned. Of course, they were imps, devils really. What else could they be?

Can you see them?

No, it's dark.

Can you smell them?

She hadn't tried.

Can you hear them move about?

She hadn't thought to.

Are they real?

She heard them, heard them all the time, with their giggles and snicker, and snide remarks. They had to be real.

They had to be?

Ava stepped into the kitchen and thought a moment. Did the imps have to be real? No, she had not glimpsed them, not really. But she had heard them. She had been attacked by them. They had fiddled with the lights. Besides, if they weren't real, what were they? Her imagination? Her imagination hadn't knocked the teapot off the counter or tripped her in the bedroom. So, they had to be real.

Didn't they?

She edged along the counter to the drawer where she kept the torch. She pulled it out and flicked the switch.

Nothing happened.

She shook the torch and tried several times, but it wouldn't come on.

The batteries are dead.

Too bad.

"They're not dead," Ava said. "I put new ones in just before I moved."

Maybe someone left it on when they put it in the drawer.

That happens.

"No, I didn't. I distinctly remember putting the torch in, and it was off." Ava stopped. "Which one of you did it?"

Laugh.

Laugh.

Ava stared, trying to locate the imps. She could hear them. Were they in the pantry? The basement? They had to be close.

"Where are your parents?" Ava asked.

Oh, they're dead.

Pity.

A cold fear raced through Ava. What was going on? Who was she talking to? How had they gotten into the house? Why couldn't she see them? The torch shook in her hand. She tried to think. The wine had some effect, as did the pain pill. Her brain didn't want to function correctly. She moved along the counter, fighting the panic growing inside her. She glanced down and noticed the blood on her arm. She needed to fix that. But she had the idea that if she tried, those two...whatever they were, would do something to stop her. She reached the end of the counter. The pantry door was only a few feet away, but two steps were required, two steps without something to hold onto.

Can you make it?

Laugh.

"I can make it," Ava said. "You think you're clever, but you're not. I'll make it."

She thought a second and lowered herself to the tile floor. On hands and knees, she smiled at no one she could see. Then, she crawled to the pantry door, the torch still in one hand. She pulled herself erect and grinned, feeling very good about her solution.

"Didn't see that coming, did you?" She opened the pantry door and reached in to turn on the light. She was happy to see it worked. But she had a horrible suspicion that as soon as she stepped inside, all the lights would go out. And she still didn't have a working torch. Although, she knew there were fresh batteries in the pantry, on the back shelf. She looked inside and the back into the kitchen. She had to get her bearings before she went for the batteries. She needed to be sure she could manipulate them in the dark.

She unscrewed the bottom of the torch and dropped out the batteries, hearing them clatter on the floor. Then, she screwed on the bottom, but not all the way. Looking into the kitchen, she backed into the pantry, one hand on the shelves.

The lights went out.

Ava didn't panic. She had expected this. She continued to back into the pantry, ready to battle anyone that might come at her. She reached the end of the shelves and reached along until she found the spare batteries.

She unscrewed the bottom and placed it on a shelf. Then, she loaded the batteries, precisely as they had come out.

She didn't see the bottom of the torch fly off the shelf.

She heard it smack the wall and hit the floor.

Oops.

Giggle.

Ava fought the urge to scream. She told herself to be calm. Nothing had changed, not really. It was dark, and she needed the bottom of the torch, and it was in the pantry with her, and the pantry was as a small room, and she should be able to find it, and...

Her lips quivered. Her foot throbbed afresh. Blood oozed out the cut on her arm. Holding the torch and keeping the batteries inside, she lowered herself to the floor. She would hand search the small room. In time, she was certain she would find the cap for the torch, and then, she would be just fine. It was simple, really. She would move from one direction to the other. If she were methodical, she would find what she was looking for. In fact, she didn't even have to use her hand. She could use the torch to rake back and forth. She felt to one corner and slowly began to work across the room. She was careful to reach under the bottom shelf, in case the cap had rolled away.

She moved to the side and then started the return. Her arm and foot hurt, but she concentrated on finding the cap.

You like sketti?

Yum-yum.

Ava heard something scrape, and for a moment she couldn't figure it out.

Then, the jar hit her in the shoulder, bouncing off, and shattering on the floor.

Ava yelped, the pain ripping through her shoulder. What the bloody hell was that? Then, she smelled the spaghetti sauce. A jar of spaghetti sauce had shattered? The pantry floor was littered with glass and spaghetti sauce?

You forget veggies?

Ava had no idea what hit her in the head. All she knew was that she saw stars, just before she collapsed. Lying on the floor, her head spun. She had the sudden realization that she was about to black out.

You hit her in the head.

Good aim, aren't I?

Giggle...giggle...giggle.

Ava heard no more.

When Ava opened her eyes, she found light filling the kitchen.

Morning.

She blinked and tried to rise. Her head spun, and she decided she needed to rest for a moment. The pain wasn't terrible, but it was enough. She raised her arm and looked at the scabbed over cut. She remembered how she got that—the wine glass. She looked about at the shattered jar and its pool of red spaghetti sauce, with grey mushrooms.

Not far from the sauce a huge can of carrots had rolled against a wall. Ava assumed that the carrots had hit her head and knocked her unconscious. She turned her head and saw a sack of flour had been emptied on the floor. Written in the flour was a simple message…

PLAY

She had to think a moment before she remembered why she was on the floor. She was looking for the cap to the torch. She had the torch when hit with the can. But now she couldn't see it. That seemed odd. She slowly rotated her head, mindful of the pain that came with movement. That was when she spotted the torch cap that she had been looking for when she blacked out. While she no longer had the torch, she would keep the cap. The torch couldn't be far away.

She put the cap into her pocket, wishing she had done that the night before. Then, she slowly climbed to her hands and knees. Her foot burned, and she remembered that she had stitches in it. Where were here pain pills? She would find them. She moved into the kitchen, which look fine to her. At least, there wasn't a lot of glass to avoid.

Crawling to the fridge Ava pulled herself erect. The room swam for a moment, but she managed to stay upright. She opened the fridge and pulled out a bottle of water guessing that water would do better than tea, although she would sooner have tea. As she sipped water, she wondered what had become of her mobile. She would find it. When she did, she would call in sick, because she really was sick. As soon as she did that, she was going to shower. She needed to clean up her arm before she bandaged it. She touched her head and felt the lump, the painful lump.

Those bloody imps.

She knew, knew they were still in the house. As soon as she found her footing, she was going to hunt them down, and when she did, there would be hell to pay.

If they were real.

Ava was pretty sure they were real. The lump on her head said they were real. And they had stolen her torch. She was going to find that too. She would need it once the sun went down, because the lighting was unreliable.

Where was her mobile?

She limped along the counter, still not sure she wanted to cross any open area. Holding onto the water, she managed to reach her bedroom. There, she found her purse...and her mobile. She opened the mobile and called her boss. She needed to check in. That was when she found out that she wasn't expected in the office.

Why not?

Because the government had ordered a lockdown. No one was going anywhere. She was going to work from home.

Alone with the imps.

Chapter Eight

The shower worked wonders. The tea, laced with pain pills, rejuvenated Ava, giving her the energy to clean up the pantry. It took double the time it should have, as Ava had to pause at times to keep from toppling over. Why was spaghetti sauce so sticky? Still, she managed. After the pantry, she took the time to clean her bedroom, finding the wine glass stem she had tossed away the night before. When she picked it up and noticed the dried blood, she looked at her arm and its bandage. The imps had much to pay for.

Imps.

Were they imps?

She was certain they were, and they were very clever. But she was going to find them.

What if they weren't real?

Then, what could they be?

Ava couldn't answer that.

Where could they be?

Ava was a bit more sure about that.

The attic.

The middle of the afternoon had arrived before Ava felt strong enough to go after the imps. She didn't have a torch, but she hoped she didn't need one. She stopped in the pantry and put fresh batteries in her pockets. She intended to find her torch sooner or later. When she did, she would have a potent weapon. She added a candle to her back pocket, along with matches. Backup. She wasn't going to tackle the imps in the dark, and it would be dark soon enough.

***

In her bedroom, Ava dressed in jeans, sweatshirt, and boots. She wasn't going to make the same mistake again. When she looked at herself in the mirror, she was stunned. She looked nothing like the vibrant, confident woman she had been. She looked older, paler, scared, very scared.

She looked at her hands, and they shook in front of her. That wasn't good, not good at all. In fact, she felt a sudden fear explode through her. She couldn't do this. She wasn't equipped to do this. The imps, well, the imps weren't human. She had to recognize that. No matter how bravely she spoke, she was scared all the way to her toes. She should leave, just go. She knew someone she could stay with, didn't she? All she had to do was make a call. There was no good reason to battle the imps. She should make the call.

Ava pulled out her mobile and made the call.

Manda was the first name on her list—and the last.

"I would love to have you for a few days, but I can't," Manda said. "We're under a lockdown. No one can move in with anyone else. We all have to stay put. Haven't you been watching?"

Ava had to admit that she had been busy with other things. She put down the phone and thought a moment. If everyone was in lockdown then no one would take her in. Neither could she go to some inn or hotel. She was stuck—unless she wanted to stay in her car. No, she wasn't about to do that, unless she absolutely had to. She made a fist and hit her thigh. She didn't want to go after them, but if she didn't, they would come after her. She was certain of that. They were mean and nasty and clever. She had the cuts and lumps to prove that.

"Oh, god," Ava said out loud. "Oh, god."

She looked out the window, noting how many hours she had left before night fell.

Not enough.

That was the message from the sun. Not enough hours in the day.

She turned away from the window. If she had to do it...

Did she?

She wondered. Could she shut herself in a room? In the basement? Some place where the imps couldn't find her?

No, they would find her. They would find her and torture her, because that's what children did. They had no adult brakes. They did whatever came to mind, like hitting someone in the head with a can of carrots.

She had to fight...or let them drive her to insanity or worse.

Ava left the bedroom and headed for the attic access. She wondered if she needed a weapon. Could she hurt them? She wasn't sure about that, but she would try. When they appeared, she would get them. More, she would destroy their attic, their place. She would do to them, what they had done to her. At least, she was going to try. She stepped into the closet and looked at the door that didn't look like a door. She really, really, really didn't want to open that door. Even as she reached for the knob, her mobile chirped. She looked at the caller.

Archie. She answered the call.

"Hey Ava! I was going to come out and do this face to face," Archie said. "But you know the government. They get in the way of everything."

"I agree. I'm afraid I'm not read up on this virus thing. Is it real?"

"Well, yeah, I mean, it's in some of the cities up north, and they're trying to flatten the curve or something by keeping us all inside."

"Flatten the curve? What's that mean?"

"Something about the hospitals and ventilators. It's over-kill as far as I'm concerned. . Hardly anyone here has anything." Archie cleared his throat. "But that's not why I called. I called to apologise. I was a little rough last night. And while I won't take credit for the doll's head, I will say I might have missed it. In any case, I don't want something like this to kill whatever we might have going."

Ava was pretty certain they had nothing going, but she was willing to accept his apology.

"I understand," she said. "And I don't blame you. There is something wrong about this house. I'm not certain what it is, but it's bad, perhaps dangerous."

"I'm not sure I understand. Something wrong with the house? Wiring or something?"

"That's part of it. It's a strange place. Lights work sometimes and not others. There are voices that I think come from the telly. It's, it's disconcerting."

"Well, if you want, I can drive out. I mean, I can because I'm an essential worker and we can't let some bloke in London tell us how to live our lives."

"Exactly right." Ava felt relief tingle in her belly. "So, you're coming out? I was thinking we should check out that attic together. That way we won't get our wires crossed."

"Works for me. I'll bring me tools. As soon as I shower."

"I'll be waiting. And, Archie, this isn't an invitation for sex, all right?"

"Of course not, of course not. I just like your company. I'll be out in a jiffy."

"I'll be here."

Ava killed the connection and backed out of the closet. For a moment, she felt a sense of hope. She wouldn't be going after the imps alone. Archie was big and strong, and she guessed he would be a great help.

Together, she thought they were enough to handle the imps, no matter what the imps were. She headed for the kitchen.

She would ease her anxiety with a glass of wine. She smiled with a sudden confidence. She had help, a sidekick, someone who would be brave no matter what. The sides were even, two on two. That alone made her feel better.

She sat at the table in the kitchen and sipped red wine. She wondered if Archie was really an essential worker or if he was breaking the law by coming over, but she didn't care. She needed help, and Archie was help. They would go from there. She put her mobile on the table. It wouldn't be long. She was tempted to call out to the imps and tell them about her help, put a little fear in them. But she resisted the urge. She thought it would be more powerful as a surprise. Perhaps that would shrink the imps' mojo. Yes, she would keep her surprise in her pocket.

Giggle.

Giggle.

Ava turned her back to the wall and looked around. She didn't see them, but she felt them. They were near. They were waiting too.

For darkness.

Ava had finished the wine before Archie rang the bell. With a smile at the imps, wherever they were, she limped to the door. When she opened it, she saw Archie's smile fade a bit. He was expecting a goddess, not a wreck.

"Come in, come in," Ava said.

"I...I brought tools." He held up a toolbox. "We'll get to whatever is ailing your electrical system."

"That's great," she said. "Can I get you a pint or something?"

"A pint would taste great. Then, we're off to that attic, right?"

"That will work."

"What's wrong with your leg?" Archie asked as he followed her.

"I stepped on a shard of porcelain," Ava answered. "In the dark, so no, I didn't see it."

"I guessed that."

"And I have a lump on my head from a falling can of carrots, a bruise on my shoulder from a jar of spaghetti sauce that shattered on the floor, and a cut on my arm from a wine glass that broke when I fell."

"My god, you're a walking trip to hospital."

"I am."

"So, how did this all happen?"

"You don't want to know."

"But I do."

"Well, to begin with, it was all in the dark, or most of it in the dark. When you can't see, you make some rather awful mistakes."

Ava handed Archie a pint and explained how she managed to have so many mishaps in a single day. He sipped and listened, and she had the feeling his estimation of her was dropping by the second. She left out the parts about the imps. She was leery about that admission. That might make him think she was bonkers and not exactly a "catch". She was apt to agree with him.

"It's time," she said. "You ready?"

"Let's do this," he said. "And when I'm done, I'll take a look at your foot. We need to make sure you don't get an infection."

"I'm all for that," she said and limped out of the kitchen.

"Wait," he said and headed for the basement. "I have to check the breakers first."

Ava followed Archie down the steps and across the basement. He opened the breaker panel and took a minute to make sure none of the breakers had tripped.

"Always start at the source," he said. "If that's good, you can begin your trace."

"We're good?" she asked.

"We're good. Let's go."

She led him out of the basement and to the second floor, the hidden door to the attic. He opened it, and she followed him up the steps. He stopped just off the stairs, and she joined him. Both had never seen anything like what greeted them.

Twenty doll's heads hung from the rafters. They were of various sizes and colours, with all manner of hair and eyes. No bodies, just heads, staring in all different directions.

"What the bloody hell," Archie said.

"I...I wasn't expecting this," Ava said.

Giggle.

Giggle.

"What was that?" Archie asked.

"You heard it too?"

"I bloody well did. Where are they?"

"I don't know," she said. "They seem to be all over."

"Two?"

"I think so. Those are the ones I've heard."

Archie looked at her. "This is a bit above my pay scale. How..."

"I'm not sure. But I'm guessing we have to take these down."

Ava looked around. "I'll get the stepladder."

Archie put down his toolbox and pulled out a sharp cutter. "I'll start with the heads. My god, Ava, this is bloody spooky."

"That's the least of it. They talk sometimes too."

Ava limped down the stairs to the bedroom and grabbed the stepladder that Archie had left there from his last visit. She lugged the short ladder up the steps and into the attic.

"Here it is," she said...right before she...

SCREAMED.

Chapter Nine

Archie was hanging from a rope, kicking his feet and trying to loosen the rope around his neck. She could see from his blue lips that he needed oxygen quickly. Yet, all she could seem to do was stare. He looked at her, and his face twisted. He needed her to do something.

But what?

His cutter was on the floor beneath his swinging boots, but that wouldn't do her any good. She couldn't reach the rope that choked him. Then, she remembered the stepladder in her hands. She quickly unfolded it and placed it under his feet.

"Step on it," she said, not quite sure he was capable of doing anything. When he didn't move, she placed his boots on the stepladder and pushed him up. Still, she didn't hear the gasp, she wanted to hear. Desperate, she grabbed his cutter and climbed the stepladder. Even as she did, a doll head flew at her. She managed to bat it away before it could wrap itself around her neck. That initiated a wicked attack from the heads, coming at her from all directions, trying to wrap around her neck.

Laugh.

Laugh.

I'll do her first.

No, I will.

Ava slashed and batted at the heads, mindful that Archie was dying right next to her. And it was as she cut two heads down, that the others suddenly stopped. They swung to and fro, but they didn't attack. Panting she looked about before she stepped higher and sliced through the rope that held Archie. He hit the floor with a loud THUMP and didn't move.

Ava half slid down the ladder, landing hard on her bad foot and YELPING at the pain. She felt to her knees beside Archie and tried to loosen the rope that had bitten into his neck. It was too tight, and she didn't have time to fiddle with it. She grabbed the cutter and carefully began to cut, she hoped far away from some vital artery or vein. She managed to nick him only twice before the rope came free.

He still didn't breathe.

"Come on," she said. "Come on."

She did the only thing she could think to do. She made a fist and hammered his chest as hard as she could.

Archie GASPED.

That was a good sign.

"Breathe, Archie," she said. "Just breathe."

He breathed and coughed, his eyes slowly coming back into focus. His neck bled a little (not much), and the rope burn was prominent.

"I..." he rasped.

"Don't try to talk," she said. "I think we need to get out of here for a bit."

He nodded.

"Can you stand?"

He nodded again.

She helped him to his feet, and together, they started for the door.

Don't you want to play?

Laugh.

Laugh.

Ava wanted to tell the imps that they would be back, but she wasn't at all sure that would happen. More, she didn't want to warn them. Not that they wouldn't know.

In the kitchen, Ava handed a pint to Archie, who had his colour back, although he looked decidedly the worse for wear.

"What?" he rasped.

"Don't talk. That's what I've been fighting for two days. They wrapped the rope around your neck, didn't they?"

He nodded.

"They're evil and cruel. And I think they get their power from the doll heads. So, we have to get rid of those. Up for it?"

He hesitated before he nodded. She could tell that he really didn't like what they were doing. It wasn't the duty he had signed up for.

"Can we do it?" he asked.

She nodded. "I think so. We have to be careful. I was stupid to leave you alone."

He sipped the pint, and she noticed a change in him, a firmness. He wasn't going to be run off...not yet.

She looked out the window, and she noticed the dusk. Night was not far off, and in the dark, she and Archie would have a harder time of it.

"Where is your torch?" she asked.

He pointed up. "Toolbox."

"They're worse in the dark, so we have to get the torch. Do you understand?"

"Go."

"No, we have to go together. You saw what happened when we were separated."

He stared at her.

"Come on." She pulled him to his feet. "Where are your keys?'

He pointed up.

"Bloody damn," she said. "We need those. In case, we have to leave."

He nodded, and she helped him to his feet.

"Scared?" she asked.

He nodded.

"Me too." Ava retrieved a sharp knife from a drawer. "For the rope," she said.

Ava trailed Archie up to the attic door. The lights were still on, and that was a bonus. He hesitated in front of the door, like someone who was thrown from a horse. Getting back in the saddle was never an easy thing.

"The quicker we do this," Ava said.

"I know, I know." He touched his neck. "You won't leave me alone, will you?"

"No, we're in this together. Before it gets dark."

Archie grabbed the doorknob and pulled open the door. He took a deep breath and started up. Ava limped behind.

Oh, goody, playmates.

Archie stopped. "I…I don't like this," he said.

"I don't either," Ava said. "Come on. Let's go."

They reached the top and the room filled with doll heads, slowly twisting at the end of the old ropes that held them in place. They both spotted the bloody cutter Archie had pulled from his toolbox. Ava looked out the window. The dark was not far off, and the dark was not their friend.

"I'll get the torch." She handed him the knife. "Get started."

He approached the first doll head slowly, mindful of the other doll heads that had all turned to watch. It was as if they were some kind of creepy audience, intent on some sort of show.

"Creepy," Archie rasped.

"Very," Ava said.

She went to her knees by the toolbox and pawed through the contents. Even as she did, Archie cut off a doll head.

The other heads SCREAMED, in twenty different voices. Ava froze, her skin crawling, fear racing through her body.

"Bloody hell," she said and looked at Archie. "I can't find it."

Giggle.

"It there," he managed to say and threw the doll's head across the room.

"I hope so."

Maybe it is, and maybe it's not.

Ava glanced at the window. She knew, knew that as soon as it was half dark, the lights in the attic would switch off. Then, she and Archie would face the imps with nothing but her...candle. She remembered she still had the candle and matches. That might help.

Archie grabbed a second head and sliced through the rope.

The other heads SCREAMED.

Ava grabbed the cutter and got to her feet. "It's not there. We have to hurry."

She grabbed a doll's head, and it bit her. "Bloody hell." She looked at her hand at the small teeth marks, the bit of blood. She looked at the doll's face, its lips smeared with red blood.

"It bit me," she told Archie. "Be careful."

"Gloves. Toolbox," he rasped.

She opened the toolbox and found the gloves. She put them on, as Archie carefully grabbed the doll's head from behind before he cut the rope. She grabbed the offending head and felt it trying to gnaw through the glove. She cut it free and threw it across the room. Archie did the same, and she had the idea they were going to succeed.

That was when the hammer flew through the air and hit Archie between the eyes. He stood for just a moment before he collapsed.

Bullseye.

Laugh.

Ava knelt beside Archie, whose eyes were closed. A welt had already begun to rise.

"Archie, Archie," she said. "Archie!"

He was unconscious.

Ava wanted to cry. Archie was far too large for her to carry down the steps, and she couldn't leave him. She knew that once it got dark, the imps would attack with all manner of things—doll heads, rope, whatever tools they had stolen from the toolbox. She had no torch, and she was pretty sure, her candle wouldn't last long. She shivered, unable to even think. She desperately wanted to run, but running was impossible.

If only he was awake.

He could hear her scream.

Ooooo, yes...screams.

The doll heads let out their inhuman screams, and Ava covered her ears. The cacophony of strident voices seared her brain. She couldn't think. She couldn't react. She was lost, her foot aching, her shoulder almost useless, her arm throbbing. And they wanted her to scream.

What do you think, screwdriver?

Should work.

"NO!" Ava yelled. But she was too late. A large screwdriver flew past her and THUNKED into Archie's side. He made no sound, not even when she jerked out the bloody screwdriver and tossed it across the room.

Nice throw.

Laugh.

Ava understood. She and Archie would be subjected to a steady barrage of tools and heads and whatever the imps could find to throw. She would soon be lying next to Archie, her body punctured by whatever was around.

I bet she leaves him.

You think she's that smart?

Laugh.

The lights went out. Weak twilight leaked through the window. Ava looked around, her heart beating fast, her mouth dry. She didn't like this, not one bloody bit.

You can leave him.

We'll take care of him.

Giggle.

Ava shook from toes to nose. She could leave him. She really could. After all, he was unconscious and too big to carry, and it would be dark soon, and she needed to save herself. Anyone could see that.

No one would fault her for that.

She didn't have a torch, and she had been beaten and bloodied.

No one would blame her.

The imps, the imps were too powerful, too evil.

No one would find fault with her.

Go on.

While you can.

Laugh.

"Leave us ALONE!" Ava yelled. "LET US GO!"

But you came to play.

Playmates.

"No, no, we didn't," Ava said. "So, we have to go."

You cut off our beautiful heads.

Beautiful heads.

"We'll put them back. I promise."

I don't think so.

Not in the dark.

Laugh.

Ava looked around. She had to escape. She had to leave Archie. But she couldn't leave him. He had come to help, and they had attacked him. She looked at his side, where the screwdriver, puncture wound bled slowly. She wondered if Archie had had his tetanus booster. Then, she found that thought odd. She needed to get him out of there. She needed light. She looked around for the missing torch. It wasn't in sight. She did the only thing she could think to do. She pulled out her candle and matches and lit it.

Feeble.

Worthless.

Candles burn fast.

The doll heads LAUGHED.

Ava jumped, so afraid, she thought she might wet herself.

Then, she stood and held out the candle. "Like fire?"

She got no answer.

Ava stepped forward and lit the hair on a doll head. The dry hair flamed immediately, melting the plastic face, setting the old, frayed rope on fire. As Ava watched, the doll face warped and melted. Even the eyes caught fire. For some reason, she found it incredibly satisfying.

No fair.

She can't do that.

Ava set another head on fire, even as the first head was suspended from what looked like pure flame. If Ava hadn't been so scared, she might have found it beautiful, artistic.

Stop it!

No fair!

The heads SCREAMED in unison, even as Ava set fire to another head. The flames were like shafts running straight to the old, dry rafters.

That was when the heads pelted her, flying off their ropes and pummelling her. She didn't stop them. She was too busy lighting ropes. It wasn't until a head bit into her neck that she paused, snatching away the little beast and holding it to the candle. Its hideous SCREAM filled the room, a room quickly filling with smoke.

NO FAIR!

YOU CAN'T DO THAT!

Ava wasn't about to stop. Mindful of the screwdriver, she moved along, lighting the heads and ropes, until the room was filled with fire that licked at the rafters. She looked up and knew the fire would soon eat through the rafters and roof, and when that happened the whole house would go up in flames.

The hammer THUNKED off her side. She heard a rib crack or break or something. But she didn't care. She grabbed the hammer and hurled it through the window. The glass broke, and fresh oxygen gusted into the room, feeding the flames.

NOOOOOOOOO!

GET HER!

More than half the ropes were on fire. The rafters were burning. She coughed as she knelt by Archie. She slapped him hard, very hard. His eyes blinked.

97

"We have to go," she said. "Get up."

He continued to blink.

She stood and grabbed his arm. "Come on. The house is on fire!"

She doesn't play fair.

Not fair at all.

Some life came to Archie, and she managed to get him to his feet, even as flaming doll heads dropped to the floor. She put his arm over her good shoulder and walked him to the steps.

"We have to go down," she said. "Help me."

"Right," he rasped.

The trip down the steps was something out of Dante's Inferno. Behind, the rafters and wood crackled and popped. Ahead, air rushed past them, drawn by the fire. Ava had never been in a fire before, but she knew they were incredibly dangerous. She had to keep Archie moving. As they reached the bottom, the door SLAMMED shut.

"No," Ava said. "No."

She tried the door, but it wouldn't budge. She knew she wasn't strong enough to open it.

"W...what?" Archie slurred.

"We have to push it open," she said. "On the count of three, we hit it with our shoulders."

"Right."

Ava counted. "One, two, now!"

Pain howled through her shoulder and up her spine, as she and Archie pushed. For a moment, they saw space, but the door shut again. She panted. Hearing the fire eating away at the attic scared her more than she could stand. She knew that she and Archie would soon be too exhausted to open the door.

"One more time," Ava said. "We have to do this."

"Right." Archie sounded a bit more engaged.

"One, two, now!"

They hit the door a second time, and the pain rocketed through her. Yet, they managed to shove it open. Like a rubber band snapping, the door slammed into a clothes rack.

"Come on," Ava said.

They limped through the closet and bedroom and into the dark hall. Ava had one thought, and that was to get out. She didn't care about anything else. Not her clothes or purse or keys or anything. They had to get out.

They don't play fair.

We hate them.

Ava hurried the best she could down the hall to the steps. In the dark, helping Archie, it wasn't as fast as she wished. Yet, she found the steps and grabbed the railing.

"Stairs, Archie. Go slow. We can't see."

Archie mumbled something unintelligible, which caused Ava to wonder if he was getting worse. The hammer blow had done some damage.

From the dark, a flaming doll head appeared and hit Ava in the chest. It bounded off and rolled down the steps, like some weird little torch.

"Oh, god," she said, even as a second head hit Archie, and this one stuck. Ava had to give up her grasp of the railing to slap away the burning head. It bounced away, and Ava knew more were coming.

Half a dozen flaming heads pelted them. She could feel the tiny teeth of the heads biting into her sweatshirt, like burrs in the forest. And she managed to swat them away, where they joined the others at the bottom, catching the carpet on fire and creating a horrible stench.

"Hang on," she told Archie. "We have to go faster."

Ava took two quick steps before Archie missed a step and tumbled down the steps and into the fire at the bottom.

"No! Oh, god, no!" she said as she hurried to him.

On her knees, she rolled Archie out of the flames. Luckily, his clothes had not caught fire, and she grabbed his arm again.

"Up, up, up," she said and pulled.

Archie gained his feet.

I hate them.

Kill them.

She looped his arm over her decent shoulder. "This is it, Archie. We have to get outside."

He didn't answer.

While the smoke and fumes worsened, the fire actually aided her. She could see the door. She could see the escape.

Half a dozen flaming doll heads hammered the door; two managed to cling. Flames licked up the door, stopping Ava in her tracks. For a moment, she just stared. What was she to do?

There was no choice. She had to keep going. They had to get outside.

She went as fast as she dared, as fast as Archie's bumbling feet allowed. She reached the door, her hand stretching for the doorknob.

She YELPED, as she touched the hot metal. To grab the knob was to burn her hand. She immediately pulled down her sleeve over her hand and grabbed the knob. Heat and pain shot through her hand, but she didn't stop. With a YELL, she pulled open the door, and a rush of cool air flowed over her.

Almost falling, she pulled Archie out of the house. She managed to get him some feet away before he lost consciousness, and she had to lay him down in the grass. She turned to the house, even as flames shot out the roof, lighting up the night sky.

Several burning doll heads flew out the door, but as soon as they left the house, they lost all power and dropped to the grass.

No FAIR!

I feel different.

Me too.

Bad.

Very bad.

Ava stared, even as the door slammed shut. She didn't care. She knew they were safe. She also knew the fire brigade would soon arrive. They would have questions, and she would explain about the shorts in the wiring. That would be enough. She had no idea how much Archie would remember. No matter. She didn't believe he would bring up doll heads and children's voice.

NOOOOOOOOOO! COME BACK!

Ava smiled.

Epilogue

"I suppose it's for the best."

Ava looked over at her ex-landlady. They stood before the cold remains of what had been the rental house. They were separated by a good ten feet, per the instructions from the government. No close contact.

"Why is that?" Ava asked.

"It was always a bit off, if you know what I mean. Little things. Gremlins, I think they're called. One of the tenants said there were lost souls in the house. Of course I never believed it"

"Lost Souls? And you didn't tell me?"

"Well, renters would complain of things being lost or moved. Two said they heard voices, children's voices. Of course, that was all imagination, or perhaps trying to get cheaper rent"

"I'm not certain of that," Ava said. But the landlady ignored her.

"But it's not a total loss. The insurance will pay for a new house, and well, those pesky lights that go off without notice will be replaced by reliable wiring."

"You're going to rebuild, then."

"Of course, but not till after this awful pandemic ends. You need a place to stay?"

"I have a friend who will take me in."

"That's fortunate. Well, I'm off. I'm glad you're not badly hurt."

"Just some cuts I have to attend to. After you rebuild, will you rent?"

"I intend to. Should I contact you?"

"Don't call me, I'll call you." Ava said as limped away from the destruction and climbed into her car. She had an appointment to remove her sutures, and she knew she couldn't miss it.

***

Ava sat on the examination table, as the nurse removed the sutures.

"You know," the nurse said, "I wouldn't be able to do this if I hadn't put them in myself. She wore a contamination suit over her clothes, complete gloves, mask, and shield. She looked like something from some Armageddon movie.

"I know," Ava said. "The virus. It's played havoc with you, hasn't it?"

"For real. There's not much I can do here. If they're really bad, I send them on to the ICU. If not so bad, I send them home and tell them to remain isolated until we get the results of the testing"

"Overwhelmed?"

"Not yet. But we're only testing the ones who complain of symptoms. And many of those have something else. It's a mess."

"How does it look?" Ava asked.

"Very good. You'll have a scar that no one will see. That's fortunate."

"Do you like puppets?" the nurse asked.

"Puppets?"

"My daughter's birthday, and I was leaning toward a doll, but dolls are so common, aren't they? I thought a puppet might be something a bit more unique."

Ava shivered. "I…I used to think dolls were nice, but I've changed my thinking. IN fact, I'm not sure I'd like a puppet either, or even a teddy bear."

"Teddy bears?"

"What about a puppy? Would your daughter like a puppy?"

"She would adore one. But puppies come with all sorts of work. She's not that responsible."

"If your daughter has a computer of some sort, you might find some sort of virtual doll or puppet app. That way, she can give herself a new doll whenever she tires of the old one."

"That might work. But it's not the same as a real puppet, something you can take to bed."

"Is she an only child?"

"No, she has an older brother."

"An app would keep her brother from hanging the doll in the attic."

The nurse stopped and stared at Ava.

"Brothers do that sometimes," Ava said.

"That would be wicked."

"Very wicked."

Ava left the building and slipped into the car.

"All go?" Archie asked.

"All go," she answered.

He started the car. "I got a call from the insurance blokes. They wanted to know how the fire started."

"And what did you tell them?"

"A bit of faulty wiring. Got too hot and, well, that happens."

"Exactly. I want to thank you again for letting me quarantine with you."

"The least I could do. You saved me life."

"I think we saved each other."

The car darted off, and Ava stared out the window at the passing buildings. She wondered how many had attics. She wondered how many attics had secrets. Too many.

The End.

I hope that you enjoyed this book.

If you are willing to leave a short and honest review for me on Amazon, it will be very much appreciated, as reviews help to get my books noticed.

Over the page you will find a preview of one of my other books,

THE HAUNTING OF COVEN CASTLE

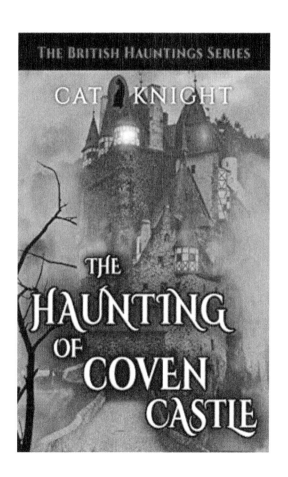

PREVIEW

THE HAUNTING OF COVEN CASTLE

CAT KNIGHT

Prologue

Coven Castle

Scotland 1802

Rowena pulled her black cloak close and pulled the hood over her head. She could hear the sleet hitting the door, and she knew that her walk would be cold and wet. Cold and wet was the usual condition in Scotland. Luckily, her walk wasn't far, less than a mile to the castle, MacDormer Castle, where Kirstine and the others waited. In private and in secret they referred to this sacred place as Coven Castle. She was proud to be asked to join the coven. Rowena had been practicing witchcraft for several years, and she had mastered a number of curses and spells. And she had managed that without being found out. Witchcraft was strictly forbidden, and those that fell under suspicion were often tried by water. Being thrown into the river with stones strapped to one's ankles was not a fair trial to Rowena's way of thinking. She knew of no spell that would keep her from drowning.

She opened the door and faced the sleet. She was happy for the filthy weather. No one would be about.

There would be no horses or carriages to avoid, no walkers to hide from. Candlelight from the cottages would not find her.

In her cloak, she was a shadow passing through the darkness. No one would know she had left her hovel. She was safe.

Rowena shivered and pulled her cloak closer. The pockets of her apron were filled with nightshade and toadstools and other ingredients that might come in handy before the night was over. Some of her treasures were in those pockets, and she was willing to share. It was the least she could do after being invited. If the coven liked her, she might be asked to replace Garia, who had been accused, tried, and burned—after her dead body was retrieved from the river. So, there was an open spot, and Rowena wanted it. Being out on such a night, with pockets filled with charms, would condemn her, if she were found out. Yet, she was willing to take the risk. As a member of the coven, she would be privy to the secrets of black magic. She would become so powerful everyone would fear her.

Coven Castle stood like a black blob in the distance. No light shone; no life could be discerned. MacDormer was no longer the citadel it had once been. The MacDormer clan had petered out except for Kirstine MacDormer, the last of the line. Barren, she was now too old to continue the lineage. Yet, Kirstine, even at her advanced age was a formidable witch. Rowena, a generation younger, was more than a bit in awe. The stories surrounding Kirstine seemed designed to create shock in anyone who might challenge her. And Kirstine had the castle, the black blob that bespoke the river of blood that some claimed had been spilt there.

The massive, oak door opened even before Rowena could slam down one of the iron knockers. She passed without a word. Her cloak was taken and hung on a peg by the door.

It was then that Rowena noticed that the witch who had met her was wearing a mask. For some reason, that struck Rowena as odd. She had not been asked to wear a mask.

The masked witch carried a single candle and led the way through the unfamiliar castle. Rowena thought she recognized the serpentine hall, designed to slow down attackers, and the great hall, where a cold draft chilled her. At that point, another door opened, and they started down curving stone steps. She thought it was another defensive mechanism. As they descended, the air grew colder. Rowena shivered, and yet, she was excited. This would be her first meeting with the coven, with the witches that ruled the village.

The room at the bottom of the steps was empty. Another candle showed that. An arrow of fear passed through her. Where were the others? She was alone with a masked witch. Rowena fought the urge to turn and run. Where were the other witches?

As if by magic, a portion of a wall opened, and the masked witch led Rowena through and into the altar room.

There were no windows in the room, which was dominated by a stone altar in the middle. Seven masked witches stood with candles, providing enough light for Rowena to see. The stone walls were dark with what could only be blood—from the bodies that had hung from the shackles attached to the stones. Had Rowena been made of weaker fiber, she might have turned and run.

But she had set her sights on being part of the coven. She would do whatever it took to win their confidence and trust.

From behind the others came Kirstine, stooped, old, yet smiling. She did not wear a mask, and she took Rowena's hands.

"Thank you for coming, Rowena. I know you have wanted to join us for some time. And now, we are able to use you."

"I am honored," Rowena said. "I will not let you down."

"I'm certain you will not. But we must be clear. You are willing to grant freedom, are you not?"

"I will do whatever is required. I seek only direction."

Kirstine turned and nodded. A masked witch stepped forward and handed Rowena a dagger, a shiny steel, black handled dagger, that looked sharp enough to cut air.

"You hold the dirk of Balem, prince of thrones and powers, tempter of wantonness. The power of Balem flows through the dirk and releases all that feel its bite. Do you believe in Balem?"

"I do," Rowena said.

"Take the dirk."

Rowena took the handle and felt a power she had never felt before.

"Feel the essence," Kirstine said. "You must be the conduit of Balem's force ."

"I feel it," Rowena said.

"Yes, my child, you feel it. You are truly the chosen one."

Kirstine waved her hand, and the other witches began to chant.

Rowena knew some Latin, but she couldn't follow what the witches sang. But she did catch the name Balem. That much was clear. They were invoking the name of Balem, the demon.

While Rowena watched, Kirstine slowly climbed upon the altar. She moaned with pain, managing to lie on her back. She pulled open her robe to bare her chest. In the scant light, Kirstine looked white and vulnerable. She waved Rowena closer.

"When I tell you. Strike fast and deep. Do you understand?"

Rowena shook her head. "No, I don't," she said.

"You must release me," Kirstine said. "The only way I can live on is if you use the dirk of Balem. You must strike. You must release me."

Rowena held up the dirk.

"The heart, Rowena, the heart."

Rowena felt the dirk. She heard the chant, the voices of the masked witches. They sang louder, the chant bouncing off the walls of the small room. She looked down. Kirstine held open her robe, her chest vulnerable. She smiled, a reassuring smile, and Rowena fought the urge to drop the dirk and run, race away.

But she couldn't run. This was her chance to join the coven, to be one of...them.

The chant quickened, and Rowena felt a rush of energy. She raised the dirk, and Kirstine smiled. It was simple really. All Rowena had to do was slam down, slam down, slam down.

Louder. Faster.

Rowena felt a huge heat fill her breast. She smiled at her own power. Yes, she could do this.

The voices filled Rowena's head. The dirk waved in the air.

"NOW, ROWENA!" Kirstine rasped. "NOW!"

Rowena struck and drove the dirk into the heart of Kirstine.

And then, things went to Hades.

Rowena's mind went black, and for some seconds, she felt completely removed from the room, the castle. She was in the land of nod. Gone.

Until she woke, and her vision cleared. She wanted to frown, but she couldn't. She wanted to speak, but she couldn't. She could do nothing but see, and to her confusion, she was looking at herself.

But that was impossible.

She couldn't be looking at...Rowena.

It couldn't be.

"Don't worry, dear," Rowena said. "It will be clear soon."

Rowena watched herself twist the dirk.

And everything went black.

READ THE REST AT THE LINK BELOW

https://www.amazon.com/dp/B086GMBQ58

HERE ARE SOME OF MY OTHER BOOKS

Ghosts and Haunted Houses: a British Hauntings Collection Sixteen books– http://a-fwd.to/58aWoW8

The British Hauntings Series

The Haunting of Elleric Lodge - http://a-fwd.to/6aa9u0N

The Haunting of Fairview House - http://a-fwd.to/6lKwbG1

The Haunting of Weaver House - http://a-fwd.to/7Do5KDi

The Haunting of Grayson House - http://a-fwd.to/3nu8fqk

The Haunting of Keira O'Connell - http://a-fwd.to/2qrTERv

The Haunting of Ferncoombe Manor http://a-fwd.to/32MzXfz

The Haunting of Highcliff Hall - http://a-fwd.to/2Fsd7F6

The Haunting of Harrow House - http://a-fwd.to/aQkzLPf

The Haunting of Stone Street Cemetery http://a-fwd.to/1txL6vk

The Haunting of Rochford House http://a-fwd.to/6hbXYp0

The Haunting of Knoll House http://a-fwd.to/1GC9MrD

The Haunting of the Grey Lady http://a-fwd.to/4EUSjb7

The Haunting of Blakely Manor http://a-fwd.to/3b2B631

The Yuletide Haunting http://a-fwd.to/7a5QF4S

The Haunting of Fort Recluse http://a-fwd.to/3Hz77IX

The Haunting Trap http://a-fwd.to/5hw7zJ8

The Haunting of Montgomery House http://a-fwd.to/20ia6sP

The Haunting of Mackenzie Keep http://a-fwd.to/7n2AWxp

The Haunting of Gatesworld Manor http://a-fwd.to/3XlZUEK

The Haunting of The Lost Traveller Tavern http://a-fwd.to/3GAG1nG

The Haunting of the House on the Hill http://a-fwd.to/1X2Wtcn

The Haunting of Hemlock Grove Manor http://a-fwd.to/LpE0k9j

The Ghost Sight Chronicles

The Haunting on the Ridgeway - http://a-fwd.to/1bGBJ6O

Cursed to Haunt - http://a-fwd.to/7BiHzLj

The Revenge Haunting. http://a-fwd.to/67V0NBO

About the Author

Cat Knight has been fascinated by fantasy and the paranormal since she was a child. Where others saw animals in clouds, Cat saw giants and spirits. A mossy rock was home to faeries, and laying beneath the earth another dimension existed.

That was during the day.

By night there were evil spirits lurking in the closet and under her bed. They whirled around her in the witching hour, daring her to come out from under her blanket and face them. She breathed in a whisper and never poked her head out from under her covers nor got up in the dark no matter how scared she was, because for sure, she would die at the hands of ghosts or demons.

How she ever grew up without suffocating remains a mystery.

RECEIVE THE HAUNTING OF LILAC HOUSE FREE!

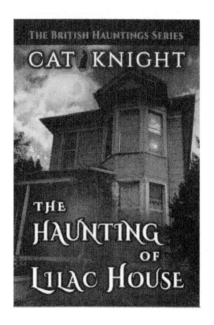

When you subscribe to Cat Knight's newsletter for new release announcements

SUBSCRIBE HERE

Like me on Facebook

Printed in Great Britain
by Amazon